SAVANNAH'S SECRET

MARIE BARTEK & THE SIPS TEAM BOOK 5

ROBIN MURPHY

Published 2021 by Next Chapter

Edited by Fading Street Services

Cover art by CoverMint

Back cover texture by David M. Schrader, used under license from Shutterstock.com

Mass Market Paperback Edition

To my mother-in-law, Mimi, who passed away during our visit to Savannah. She was a voracious reader and I hope she looks upon this book with favor.

A professional writer is an amateur who didn't quit.

RICHARD BACH

ONE

Elizabeth Tanner awoke to the sound of a squeal coming from their barn and wearily looked at her alarm clock as her blurry blue eyes read two-thirty in the morning. She slowly rolled into a sitting position and heard the squeal again. She quickly grabbed her robe as her long wavy disheveled auburn hair bounced off her shoulders.

Her thirteen-year-old petite frame cautiously tip-toed out of her bedroom and snuck past her parent's room carefully missing the creaky boards in front of their door. She descended the stairs and quickly slipped on her rain boots, grabbed a flashlight out of the junk drawer, and cautiously made her way out toward the barn.

The squealing had stopped, but she heard a strange gurgling sound just inside the opened door-way. She slowly tilted her head and leaned in as she tried to adjust her eyes to the pitch-black stable. She entered the barn and walked toward the pigs and the sound of slurping.

The moonlight shot its vibrant beam through an

opening in the ceiling, which revealed a dark figure huddled over one of the pigs in the corner of the stall. Elizabeth stood frozen until she turned and lost her balance and knocked a shovel off the wall creating a loud crash. When she shined the flashlight toward the corner of the pig stall, she saw a pair of golden eyes staring back at her. Within seconds, the figure leaped onto the wall on all fours and crawled along the ceiling, and then slithered out through the loft door and disappeared.

Elizabeth couldn't believe what she witnessed as she pointed the flashlight onto the pigs and the fluorescent beam revealed one of them covered in blood. She threw down the flashlight and ran toward the house trying to decipher what had just happened and immediately screamed out to her parents.

MARIE BARTEK-MILLER SAT cross-legged in her kitchen chair sipping her coffee as she continued to reminisce about the honeymoon pictures from France. It was a dream come true to have visited the country where her ancestors had lived. She stopped at a photo of she and Cory standing in front of Notre Dame and smiled at her six-foot-two husband looking sexy in his jeans, button-down oxford, and showing his pearly whites for the camera.

Before she swiped through to the next photo, she heard the door open from the bathroom and sensed her husband approach her from behind. Without turning around, she said, "Good morning, handsome."

Cory Miller leaned down and swiftly moved Marie's long blonde hair to the side as he brushed a light kiss on her neck. "Good morning, my wife. Are you looking at those photos again?"

"I'm dreaming of our honeymoon and how amazing it was. I also realized I need to go on a diet after all of the food I ate."

"I think we need to get that picture of us at the Eiffel Tower framed. Your eyes are particularly green in that one, and you do not need to go on a diet. With your height, you can eat anything."

"I'm only five foot seven. I may swim a few laps this morning. The ocean seems pretty calm. By the way, the coffee is on, and I was trying to decide on eggs or just a muffin." Marie felt her three-year-old chocolate lab, Bailey, nudge his wet snout on her calf. "I think Bailey's hungry too."

Cory poured his coffee and set it on the counter and proceeded to dump a cup of dog food in the large raised ceramic dish. "Gale said Bailey was great company, but he did mope around quite a bit while we were gone."

"I know, he hates it when we leave him. Speaking of which, I may take him to work with me. He loves seeing all the animals that come into the office."

Cory took a sip of the hot brew and sat down in the kitchen chair next to her. "That's the beauty of being the owner of your veterinary practice. It's going to be hard getting back into the groove of going to work after being in France for the last two weeks."

"Tell me about it. We need to have the team over for a barbecue and share our photos with them. Of course, we don't want to drag that out. I don't want to bore them." Marie chuckled.

"I think that's a great idea. Besides, you're dying to hear about the Parson investigation."

Marie grinned wide and crossed her eyes. "You know me so well. Gale said they had a great night and a ton of experiences. They caught a bunch of EVPs. Let's do it this Saturday. I'll send a group text this morning and see if everyone can make it."

Cory winked and got up from the table and walked over to the stove. "Why don't I make some scrambled eggs, and you toast us some English muffins?"

"Sounds good to me." Marie watched Bailey lap up the last of his food, and she shook her head. "Bailey's done inhaling his breakfast. Do you want strawberry or blackberry jam?"

Cory cracked the eggs into a bowl and began whisking them at a rapid pace. "Surprise me."

Marie opened the refrigerator, grabbed the blackberry jam, and set it on the counter. Before she could pop the muffins in the toaster oven, her phone rang. She glanced at the name Gale Winters and smiled, "Looks like Gale can't get enough of me."

Cory dumped the eggs into the hot frying pan and then lowered the heat. "You two are joined at the hip. I'll take over and finish the muffins. You'll be lucky if you get to eat anything after talking with her."

Marie scrunched up her nose and then tapped the green accept button and placed it on speaker. "Good morning, girlfriend, are you missing me already? You just saw us last night."

Gale's voice lazily came through the speaker. "Very funny, I was just awakened by a frantic phone call for an investigation."

"You just woke up? Gale, it's nine thirty."

"Don't lecture me, Mom. Tim and I had a late

night after we picked you up from the airport. Anyway, you're going to love this. The call was from a Mrs. Barbara Tanner. She lives in Savannah, Georgia and she believes her daughter saw a vampire. Can you believe it? A vampire? That just cracks me up."

"Okay, that's different, but what are we supposed to do about that? I mean we deal with ghost investigations. We've never dealt with vampires. What does she want us to do?"

"She wants us to go to her place and do an investigation. She claims her daughter, Elizabeth, witnessed something killing one of their pigs."

"Are you serious?"

"Yeah, and after she spotted it with a flashlight, she saw gold eyes, and then it climbed up the wall, on the ceiling, and then out of their barn loft door. Do you think the girls a little cuckoo, or was it real?"

"I'm not sure how we can help, and I have no clue if she's cuckoo. Cory and I were planning on having you and the SIPS team over this Saturday for a barbecue. I think this would be the perfect opportunity to discuss this. What do you think? Are you and Tim available?"

"Hell, yeah, Tim did his night shift stint at the firehouse last weekend. I'm always free. I can close the antique shop anytime. It's time for my margaritas and salsa dip. By the way, how's it feel to be married? Did you and Cory have a welcome home romp last night?"

Cory yelled, "That's none of your business."

"Marie, take me off the speaker. Hi, Cory, how are you?"

Marie hit the speaker button and placed it up to

her ear. "You're such a dope. Talk to Tim. We're thinking drinks at six. I'll round everyone else up. Talk to you later."

Cory placed two plates of eggs and a plate of muffins on the table. "Oh, how I've missed her crazy."

Marie smiled and said, "Yeah, me too."

"I suppose I'll have to catch up on the crazy that's been going on around here and down at the station." Cory rolled his eyes and bit into a muffin loaded with blackberry jam.

"I'm sure your deputies handled things well enough while you were gone. I think the town of Sullivan's Island survived without their chief of police." Marie winked and finished the last bite of scrambled eggs. "You make the best eggs."

"You always say that because you didn't have to make them."

"True, but they are good. I'm going to stop at the grocery store after I make my rounds today. We're out of everything. I'll need to stock up on extra snacks for our barbecue. I suspect it'll be a long night."

"I think I'm going to be late tonight. I'm sure I'll need to catch up on a mound of paperwork. No need to keep my dinner warm." Cory stood up and kissed her on the forehead.

"My dear husband, surely you know me by now. I don't make dinner, but I'll keep the take-out warm for you." Marie gathered the plates and set them in the sink.

Cory grabbed Marie around the waist and pulled her close. "I love it when you call me your husband."

Marie set her chin on his chest and looked up into his deep brown eyes. "I know, but unfortunately we have no time this morning to relish being husband and wife. Back to reality."

Cory released her grip and slapped her on the ass. "Reality sucks."

"Yes, yes it does." Marie grabbed Bailey's leash and knelt down on the floor. "Come on boy, you need your morning constitution, and we need to get to work."

Cory chuckled as Bailey's tail thumped against the floor. "He's glad to be back to reality."

Marie smiled at the motley crew surrounding the snack table in the meeting room on top of her garage. As much as she loved France and meeting her long-distance relatives, she missed this amazing group of people who have given her support with learning to understand her psychic abilities, as well as solving murders and dealing with demon possessions and the occult. There was no other place she'd rather be.

"Marie we are so glad you're both back home. We missed you and Cory." Jim Rawlings leaned his tall, thin frame against the wall as he shoved a corn chip drenched in salsa in his mouth. He smelled of mentholated cream, and his balding head glowed under the lights.

Marie replied, "Thank you, Jim. We missed all of you too. France was a dream come true, but it's always nice to come home. Anything exciting happening at the store?"

Jim owned the local Kangaroo Express and had a tender heart and was adored by the community. Some felt sorry he was married to Mimi. "No, same old thing going on, but we did hire a new clerk. Although

Mimi isn't too happy about it because she's eighteen and looks like Jennifer Lawrence."

"Oh, well good luck with that." Marie patted Jim on the shoulder and shook her head.

"Who looks like Jennifer Lawrence?" Mimi Rawlings, the local pharmacist, appeared out of nowhere wearing a powder blue sundress that showed off her recently thinner body as her wire-rimmed glasses slid down her plump nose.

Marie tried to deflect the argument that was about to ensue with Jim. "I was just telling Jim that a waitress who waited on us in France looked like Jennifer Lawrence. Mimi, you look great. You must be sticking to that diet you started before we left."

Mimi was immediately distracted by the praise as she smiled and said, "Thank you, Marie. I'm glad some of you noticed."

Jim rolled his eyes and walked away as he mumbled, "I noticed."

Marie said, "I love your hair. You got some highlights."

"Yes, I've needed a change, and I feel like a new woman. The doctor is pleased that my blood pressure is leveling, and I may be able to come off my medicine. My nutritionist has worked wonders for me." Mimi bit into a strawberry and continued chewing before she said, "We can't wait to hear about France and also to tell you how the Parson investigation went. It was a night of crazy activity."

"That's what Gale told me. We have a lot to catch up on." Marie guided Mimi over to the conference table and set her empty margarita glass down on the table.

"What did I tell you?" Gale stood next to Marie

wearing a low-cut T-shirt that read *Good Girls Do Bad Things* and jean shorts that accentuated her curvy build. Her five-inch wedged sandals had her towering over Mimi.

Marie read her shirt and raised her right eyebrow. "You go out in public with that shirt?"

"There's nothing wrong with this shirt. Tim thinks it's funny." Gale swished her long sable hair behind her back and strutted over to the pitcher of margaritas. "Marie, you look like you need a refill."

"Yes and thank you. I was telling Mimi that you told me about the Parson investigation."

Gale walked over to Marie carrying the margarita pitcher and began filling her glass. "We have lots to talk about and share. I say we get down to business."

Tim Haines walked over to Marie and said, "Welcome home again. I'm looking forward to hearing more about France." Tim's biceps hadn't shrunk any while they were in France as his shirtsleeves clung on for dear life. His fire chief hat was molded to his head and his brown military styled hair peeked out at the edges.

"It was amazing. We have pictures to share, but we'll do that after we go over your findings from the Parson's house."

"Great, is Cory coming tonight?"

"He'll be here shortly. He had an impromptu council meeting he had to attend."

"They're probably discussing the elevator installation at the station." Harry Connor slithered in on their conversation wearing his usual wrinkled suit and bow tie. His dark-rimmed glasses no longer displayed medical tape at the nose.

"Harry, how are you? Are you ready for school yet?" Marie leaned over and kissed his cheek.

Harry blushed and said, "I'm always ready for school. It's the students who aren't."

Gale smiled and let out a big sigh. "Being the guidance counselor, I would imagine you look forward to dealing with the deviants at Wando High."

"We don't call them deviants, but yes, I look forward to chatting with those who need my services."

"Ahh, Harry, always the diplomat." Gale winked and walked away from the group.

Marie placed her hand on Harry's forearm. "Ignore her, Harry. After all, look at the silly shirt she's wearing."

Gale yelled back, "I heard that."

Marie sat down at the table and began shuffling through her notebook and said, "Will Isabella be joining us tonight?"

Mimi replied, "Yes, I ran into her at the pharmacy today. She said she'd be a little late because she was dog sitting for their neighbor. They're supposed to be coming home from vacation today."

Isabella Swanson was thirteen with shoulder-length platinum hair and the newest member of SIPS. Marie had become her mentor after discovering she had psychic abilities. She blamed herself for the kidnapping of Isabella by the local professor who had decapitated three people on the island the month before. Isabella was a crucial player in helping them solve the case. She was a great addition to the team, but more importantly, she filled the void Marie had after losing *her* mentor, Myra Cummings.

"Okay, I think it's time we go over the evidence you all got from the Parson investigation, and then try to decide how we can help the Tanner family. We may be taking a trip to Savannah."

Marie watched the team gather in their seats as they pulled out their laptops and equipment and started to share their findings with Marie. She began taking notes as the buzz of their voices put a smile on her face, and she thought, yes, it's good to be home.

TWO

THE SUNDAY MORNING sunshine danced on the bedroom walls as Marie slowly woke and tried to move her leg out from under Bailey's rump. She nudged her foot and bumped Cory's back in the process with her knee. Neither stirred as Marie carefully rolled out of bed and set her feet on the floor. It was a long night of margaritas and laughter the night before, and she was still catching up on her sleep from France.

She threw on a pair of athletic shorts and a tank top and tiptoed out of the bedroom. Since it was eleven in the morning, it seemed appropriate to make brunch. As she started the coffee and began heating the pan with the bacon, she played back the findings and discussions of the Parson's investigation. The team proved there was a haunting at the Parson's house. Their evidence documented it was Tammy Parson's mother doing the haunting. Marie was glad the team was able to put her fears to rest, but it was even more inspiring how Isabella brought healing messages from Tammy's mother.

Marie mixed the pancake batter and heard a

sound from the bedroom. Bailey made his entrance into the kitchen and stood by the door waiting to relieve his bladder. Marie held the screen door open a few feet as he romped down the porch stairs and over to a palm tree.

Cory eventually made his way into the kitchen and kissed Marie's cheek and said, "Good morning. That was one hell of a night, wasn't it? It was great to be back and in the middle of conversations about ghosts, vampires, and France."

Marie flipped the bacon and then began pouring the batter into the skillet. "It was a great night. I missed those folks. Who would have dreamed that the Sullivan's Island Paranormal Society would be called on to do such great things in helping others? I was thrilled how well Isabella did. You could see how proud she was telling me about the messages she received from Tammy's mother."

Cory poured a cup of coffee, walked over to the door, and let Bailey back into the kitchen. "It was great sharing our pictures with them from France. It made me a little homesick telling them about the great food and wine we had with your cousins."

Marie flipped the pancakes and then placed the bacon strips on a plate with paper towels to catch the extra grease. She watched Cory feed Bailey as she poured herself a cup of coffee and splashed a bit of creamer into the steamy java. "My real concern is how we're going to deal with this situation for the Tanners. None of us could agree on what to do for them. Gale and Jim think it's a hoax, whereas Harry and Isabella think it's real. The rest of us were on the fence. You didn't weigh in on your opinion. What do you think about vampires feeding on pig's blood?"

Cory slid the pancakes from the skillet and onto another plate and set them in the middle of the table. "To be honest, I'm not sure. There's a part of me that just thinks the whole thing is ridiculous."

Marie sat down and began filling her plate with pancakes, bacon, and fruit left over from their meeting. "And the other part?"

Cory took a sip of coffee and looked straight into Marie's emerald eyes. "The other part of me has gotten to know how real the paranormal is and that we can't blow off someone in need of our help. I don't know if there are vampires, but I didn't believe in demons either. Look where that got us."

Marie reflected back on the loss of Myra to the demon that took her life too soon. "Yes, I agree. I think we need to help this family. If nothing else, we need to get to the bottom of what is going on at their farm. It looks like we'll have to carve out some time on our schedules and make reservations in Savannah."

"Works for me. Now that that's settled, I'd like to finish enjoying this great breakfast and sneak in some time with the morning paper."

Marie smiled and bit into a piece of bacon. "Yes, I'd say you have some catching up to do on the news. I'm going to do some yoga and meditate. I need to see if I can get anything on this vampire situation. I hope my angels can give me some guidance."

Marie completed a session of yoga and remained in the sukhasana pose and began to clear her mind to see if she could receive messages from Ladislava Maria Hynick, her fourth great-grandmother, and Ludomir Zoran Courty, the young boy ancestor. She wasn't quite sure how she was related to Ludomir, but he was always there for guidance.

After a few minutes of deep breathing and quieting her mind, she began to see a vision of fields of corn and crops. It was massive lands of green and gold, and the beauty was breathtaking. She saw Ladislava holding Ludomir's hand as they guided Marie through the fields and eventually stopped short in front of a barn.

Marie felt a chill and was guided into the barn while Ladislava and Ludomir telepathically gave her caution. They hovered in the corner and watched the scene play out with Elizabeth Tanner entering the barn and catching the horrid beast feeding on one of the pigs. Then, before the beast scurried up the wall, everything shifted into slow motion. Marie watched the golden eyes float as the creature made its way toward the loft door. Marie caught the beast's pale skin under the moonlight and two puncture marks on its neck. Before she could see anything more, the monster slipped out and disappeared into the night.

Marie telepathically asked Ladislava what the beast was and why it was feeding on the pig, to which he replied, "There is an evil element taking place in Savannah, and you must be extra cautious."

Marie then asked, "Is this indeed a vampire?"

He said, "There are both real and fictitious vampires. All are deadly. Determining the difference will be difficult. Nonetheless, they need your help. We shall be here for extra guidance and protection."

Marie wanted to ask more questions, but Ladislava and Ludomir were beginning to fade. She kindly thanked them for their direction and slowly opened her eyes and thought, "Is there such a thing as real vampires?"

She blew out her candle, walked into the kitchen,

and immediately grabbed her cell phone to dial the Tanner family. Whatever was taking place at their farm and in Savannah, she knew the Tanners needed the team's help. The next phone call would be to Gale to begin mapping out travel plans.

Serafino Petrovic leaned forward in his leather wingback chair and glared at his fledgling kneeling in front of him on the floor. He tried to remain calm as he rubbed his thumb and forefinger across his rugged jaw. His coal black hair was tied back into a ponytail, and his blood red eyes narrowed as he tried to decide how to handle the current situation.

He remained calm as a slow grin fell at the corners of his mouth. "Nicolai, you deceived me, didn't you? You went out and killed and then lied about it."

The young blond-haired Nicolai kept his head bowed and said, "No, Master, the pig was already dead."

"It doesn't matter. Someone saw you." Serafino leaned back into the chair and skillfully crossed his legs. "This will more than likely bring an investigation to our house. We do not need people snooping around our organization."

Nicolai picked up his head and tried to speak, but his voice squeaked as he said, "But I was so hungry, Master."

"You hybrid fool." Serafino slammed his fist on the table next to him as his voice bellowed through the room. "If it weren't for the promise I made your mother, I'd have killed you myself. Eat the mortal food if you're hungry. You must learn to blend in with the humans. Killing is a last resort."

Nicolai remained in a ball on the floor as his body shook. "Yes, Master, I'm sorry. Please forgive me."

Serafino looked at Despoina, one of his mistresses, and waved his hand. "Take him to his room and be sure to watch him this time. The next time he escapes, it'll be you suffering the consequence."

Marie had finished talking with Gale when her phone rang. She saw Isabella's name as she placed the phone on speaker and said, "Hi, Isabella, how are you today?"

"I'm fine, but I think I had a vision about our possible case in Savannah."

"Okay fill me in, and by the way, I think we're going to Savannah to help the Tanners. I just got done talking with Gale about arrangements. I hope you'll be able to come along."

"Oh absolutely, I can't wait."

"Great, can you explain to me what happened in your vision?"

"Well, as per usual, it doesn't make a whole lot of sense, but I had a dream of a young girl by the name of Gracie who seemed to be pleading with me to help. Not quite sure what kind of help, but she was insistent. I could see this wrought iron fence and tombstones, so I'm not sure if it was about a cemetery, or if she was showing me someone had died. She was wearing a white dress, and at times, I'd see her skipping and playing. I also got the name of Johnson. It was odd."

"The visions usually are and never make sense at

first. How are you dealing with these visions? I know it can be a scary thing at times."

"I'm okay, it does freak me out when they come out of nowhere, but you've helped me a great deal on centering myself. I'm able to calm my thoughts and stay focused."

Marie shifted in her chair and silently sighed to herself. "I'm glad. It still freaks me out too, so you're not alone in that area. Getting back to this Gracie, did you happen to get her last name?"

"Not the whole name, but I saw the letter W. So, I'm sure I'll get more as we head to Savannah. When are we going, by the way?"

"Next week, which gives you a few weeks before you have to report to school."

"That's great because I already told Mom we might be making the trip. She was okay with it but said she'd want to speak with you before we go. You know Mom."

Marie chuckled, "I wouldn't have it any other way, Isabella. Have her give me a call, and I can fill her in on what we're doing. It's perfectly understandable for her to be concerned. After all, we never know what we're dealing with until we get there."

Isabella reluctantly agreed as their conversation ended, and Marie scrolled through her contact list. She called each of the SIPS members to fill them in on the arrangements for their investigation to Savannah. Some thought it was a silly idea while others were ready to go. After a long and somewhat tedious conversation with Harry, Marie finally hung up and decided it was time for a long walk to clear her mind and get her heart rate up. Harry had a way of winding everyone up, and the best way to keep her patience was exercise.

THE SIPS TEAM met at Marie's beachfront house to unload the equipment from the meeting room into their vans and SUVs. This group was like a well-oiled machine, as they each knew what role they played in making sure they had everything needed for an investigation.

As each of them double-checked their list, Marie tightened Bailey's harness in the backseat and grabbed hold of his head and kissed his nose. "I wasn't about to leave you again, so you better get your game face on to help us in our investigation."

Gale laughed at Bailey's thumping tail on the seat. "You two are pitiful."

"I know. Besides, Bailey's part of the team."

"Mhm, well let's hope he has some insight into these so-called vampires and can prove whether they're real or not because I still say this is a wild goose chase."

"Yes, Gale, you've made that quite clear. Keep that to yourself before we get into another debate with Harry. We have roughly two hours until we get there and I'm not in the mood to listen to you two arguing...again."

Gale made a cranky face and said, "Gee, is it that time of the month? Or is married life getting to you already?"

Cory chimed in and said, "Okay girls, let's simmer down."

Marie rolled her eyes and got into the front passenger seat of Cory's SUV and said, "Oh I'm fine, just laying out some ground rules for the road."

The team settled into their vehicles, turned on their two-way radios to remain in contact on their drive, and then set off for Savannah. The weather was beautiful in August as the heat of the summer slowly dissipated. Marie was still able to strike a deal on the price of the two carriage houses, even though it was considered to be peak season.

They only needed two stops for bathroom breaks and arrived at the Tanner residence by ten a.m. Gale couldn't stop giggling at the road sign, Boykin Road, which seemed to have a similar sound to boinking. Harry wasn't amused, and Marie needed to remind Gale that there were children aboard.

They snaked up the long winding lane where green fields were exposed with goats, pigs, cows, and chickens lazily grazing and pecking amongst each other. The sun poked through the trees, and the farmhouse came into view with a large pond off to the left, which revealed ducks and geese gracefully gliding on top of the water.

Cory parked the SUV and turned off the engine. "This place is spectacular. Who would have thought all of this was tucked away back here?"

Marie got out of the SUV and stretched her back. The hat she wore exposed her dishwater blonde ponytail through the opening as it bounced off her shoulder. "This looks similar to what I saw in one of my visions last week. I'm pretty sure we're where we need to be from the guidance my angels gave me."

Each team member got out of the vehicles and began to walk around the property. Marie nodded her head at Gale to follow her to the quaint farmhouse, which was a log home with a red metal roof. The sun was warm on the skin, and the smell of nature was exhilarating.

Before they approached the steps of the porch, a woman in her fifties with chestnut hair tied back in a bun stepped out from the screen door and smiled. Her thick southern accent was gentle and sweet. "Hello, you must be the group from the paranormal team."

Marie nodded her head and gently placed her hand on the railing. "Yes, we are. My name is Marie, and this is Gale. We're the co-founders of the Sullivan's Island Paranormal Society."

Gale interjected, "SIPS for short. Are you Barbara? It's nice to meet you."

"Yes, I am. It's so nice to meet you both. Thank you for coming out here so quickly. We've been beside ourselves ever since the incident happened. My husband, Bob, thinks we're a little crazy." Barbara was the spitting image of Sandra Bullock as her teeth radiated from her smile.

Marie walked up the steps and extended her hand to Barbara. "Don't you worry about that; we love dealing with crazy."

Barbara smiled wide and shook Marie's hand. "I'm sure you do. Can I interest you and your team in some of my homemade lemonade? It's a bit early for my Chatham Artillery Punch, but I suspect ya'll would love to have some later."

Gale perked up to the reference to alcohol. "It's never too early for alcohol. It's five o'clock somewhere. Just what exactly is Chatham Artillery Punch?"

"It's got lemons, lots of sugar and brown sugar,

bourbon, cognac, a little rum, and champagne. It's delicious and very potent."

Marie glared at Gale. "It sounds delicious, but I think we will wait until later to try your recipe. Gale will be fine with lemonade for now."

Gale rolled her eyes and ignored Marie. "Yes, lemonade will be fine for now."

The group made their way up the large open porch to make their introductions and then decided to get down to business and interview Elizabeth. They wanted to hear more about her experience the night their pig got slaughtered.

During that time, Marie felt a sense of negativity and sadness and wanted to have a chat with Isabella so they could compare notes. There was no doubt in her mind there was an evil presence that had been on Tanner's land. Exactly what that presence was, was hard to figure. Whatever it was, it had Marie tense and a little nervous. She didn't like dealing with these things. The unknown always had a way of wreaking havoc.

THREE

After the interview with Elizabeth, the team began their usual routine of placing the equipment in the hot spots. Marie felt it was the perfect opportunity for her to have some alone time with Isabella to get her take on the whole situation.

Marie opened the screen door and said, "Isabella, why don't you and I go over to the pond and have a chat."

They made their way out into the warm air past the donkeys and continued to walk by the long stretch of crops planted in uniformed rows. The smell of the soil and flowers put Marie into a Zen-like state as she guided Isabella over to a couple of chairs haphazardly placed under a southern live oak.

Isabella took in a deep breath and closed her eyes as she sat down into one of the green painted vintage metal chairs. "This place is beautiful and scary at the same time."

"That's exactly why I wanted to talk to you. I'm picking up on some sadness and negativity. I sense evil and can feel there was something that happened in the barn." Marie switched her phone to vibrate and placed it in her purse and then set everything on the ground.

"I also saw that same little girl, Gracie, that I told you about before we got here. She is definitely in a panic to get my attention. I can't seem to focus on what she's trying to say. I need to switch to her vibration."

"I think it may be a good moment for both of us to quiet our minds and do a little meditation. There's a strong possibility that we'll be able to mesh our thoughts and feelings to come up with some answers."

They each leaned back into the chairs and began their process of meditation. Marie immediately saw her spirit guides and tried to take in their warnings of evil and danger, when suddenly, she spotted a young girl in a white dress impatiently tugging on her spirit guides' hands.

Marie was able to sense Isabella questioning this little girl and heard the name Gracie. Many voices were beginning to ring in Marie's ears as she tried to ask them to speak one at a time. Marie eventually heard Gracie tell Isabella that the monster with golden eyes killed the animals with their pointy teeth and scared the children.

Within minutes Gracie disappeared, and Marie focused on Ladislava's voice as she guided Marie to an Italianate style faded red brick house and picked up on the word *bull*. There were palm trees and lush gardens surrounding the house, and a wrought iron fence that encompassed the entire property. She was able to see broad overhanging eaves and round-headed windows with hood moldings.

Before Marie could learn the significance of this house, Ladislava slowly disappeared, and Marie found herself back in her chair at the farm. She opened her eyes and spotted Isabella staring at her.

"That was one hell of a vision. I was able to hear you talking with Gracie. What were you able to see?"

Isabella slowly shook her head. "I saw your spirit guide take you to a house. Where was that?"

"I don't know. We'll have to write this down in our journals while it's fresh in our minds. You know something will relate to our visions eventually. I'd like to know why I saw the word bull. Did you pick up on that?"

Isabella rapidly wrote in her journal, and then stopped short. "No, I didn't. Did you see a cemetery?"

"No, I didn't see any cemetery." Marie followed suit and began to write everything she could remember in her burgundy leather journal.

Isabella said, "I think I know the name of the cemetery. I was able to pick up the word Bonaventure. I remember reading about that on the Internet just the other day."

"Obviously, these elements tie together somehow, and the golden eyes match the description Elizabeth gave us on what she saw in the barn. Gracie called it a monster with pointy teeth. I think we're dealing with vampires. What the hell do I know about vampires?"

Isabella stopped writing and shockingly looked at Marie. "Seriously? You haven't read or watched the Vampire Diaries?"

"No, I'm afraid I haven't. As I said the other night at our meeting, I don't believe in them. But now, after both of our visions, I think I may need to bone up on some vampire history."

"Where will you do that?"

"I'm not sure. Maybe we can go to the library. It's

one thing to watch a television series, but I need to get to the real history. I may begin doing a few web searches too." Marie stood up and grabbed her purse and journal. "Come on, let's go share some of this with the team and then figure out how we can learn about what makes a real vampire tick."

Marie and Isabella joined the team and shared their visions. The skeptics still weren't convinced about there being real vampires, but they also knew not to distrust Marie's psychic ability, especially with Isabella to back them up.

Gale leaned back in the glider as she shaded her eyes from the sun. "I'm still not convinced. Personally, I think there's an explanation for your vision. How many times have you said your visions don't make much sense? It takes real deciphering to put it all together."

Harry chimed in and said, "In the eighteenth century there was an increased level of vampire superstition in Europe that led to mass hysteria. In some cases, it resulted in people jamming stakes into corpses and accusing them of vampirism."

Gale leaned forward and stared at Harry. "Are you talking about the story from Bram Stoker? Do you seriously believe in this stuff?"

"What I'm saying is, it was folklore, but if you get enough people believing in it, it becomes real. Plus, the first story titled, The Vampyre, was written by John Polidori in eighteen nineteen."

Gale sighed and leaned back into the chair. "You would know that."

Tim asked, "Harry, are you trying to say that someone is out to make it look like a vampire slaughtered the Tanners' pig?"

"It's possible."

Cory finished his second glass of lemonade and wiped the sweat from his brow. "I was thinking the same thing. You all know how I rationalize everything from a cop's way of thinking. But I also don't place any doubt in my wife's visions. I think we need to learn a little more about vampires and also to find out if anything like this has happened elsewhere."

Marie placed her journal in her purse and nodded in agreement. "That's what I said to Isabella. I need to learn more about vampires, folklore or not. I was headed to find a library. Harry, can you help me find a book on the subject? I need to get a feel for the whole story about vampirism."

Jim shrugged his shoulders and lifted out of his chair with a sigh. "I still don't believe in any of this, but I'm not going to question Marie and Isabella either. Whatever you need me to do, I'm ready to help."

"Thank you, Jim. Mimi, you're usually the one researching history for us. Can you do a little digging also? You have the natural sleuthing ability when it comes to the history of the town."

"I'd love to help. Even though it's considered folklore, there's still something mysteriously exciting about vampires. I'll find the local historical society and learn as much as I can." Mimi grabbed a grape from a bowl of fruit that Mrs. Tanner had set out and popped it in her mouth.

"Thank you, I appreciate it. Tim, can you and Jim go back in and ask the Tanners if anything like this has happened to any other animals? Also, let them know we'll be back later this evening around seven to begin our investigation." Marie looked at Isabella and placed her hand on her shoulder. "I'm sure you're not interested in going to a library and researching since you're stuck doing it in school, but I sure could use some of your insight."

"No, I think this is great. I love vampires. Besides, I'd like to do more research on Gracie."

Cory replied, "I think I need to introduce myself to the local police and see if I can learn anything from them. I'll meet you back here hopefully with some information about the Tanners pig."

Marie smiled and then addressed the group. "Sounds like we have a plan on what we all need to do next. Let's give our good wishes to the Tanners and then head out. We have a lot to do before we investigate."

Marie, Harry, Isabella, and Gale made their way to the Live Oaks Library on Bull Street to see if there were any books about possible local folklore and vampires. Jim, Tim, and Bailey stayed back with the Tanners. They needed to ask more questions and make sure all of the equipment was up and running for the investigation. Cory dropped Mimi off at the local historical society before he headed to the police station.

Gale stood frozen in the aisle marked historical fiction staring blankly at the books in front of her as she mumbled to herself. "I have no idea what the hell I'm looking for in here."

Suddenly a voice from her left said, "May I help you?"

Gale jumped and realized she said that last thought out loud and spotted a plump woman in her fifties looking at her with a jovial smile and pink cheeks. "Oh, I'm sorry, I didn't mean to say that out loud."

"That's quite all right. Is there something in particular that you're looking for?" The woman slowly approached Gale and routinely began to slip books back into their proper places on the shelf.

"Yes, there is. My friends and I were wondering if you had any books on local folklore, such as vampires or anything in that realm."

"Oh yes, we have a local author section with books on ghosts and local folklore. If you head out to your left and make your way to the end of this aisle, you'll see a very tall potted Kentia palm tree. The section you are looking for is to the right of that plant. You can't miss it."

"Thank you very much." Gale smiled at the sweet librarian and made her way toward a plant she had never heard of before and then turned right only to find everyone sitting around a table with their noses in books. "Oh nice, you could have let me know you were all here."

Marie casually glanced up over a local author's ghost book and said, "I just figured you were in the children's or magazine section."

"Very funny, I was looking in the historical fiction section but started to doze off when a very nice librarian pointed me in this direction." Gale grabbed a chair from another table and slid it next to Isabella. "What have you all found out so far?"

Isabella shrieked and then caught herself and spoke in a whisper. "I found the story on Gracie. Her last name is Watson. I think she's the one who came to me in my vision. It says here that she died of pneumonia at the age of six. Her parents and the town of

Savannah were heartbroken. Her father had a sculpture made of her, and it is at her gravesite in the Bonaventure Cemetery. Her father quit his job, and then they moved back to New England leaving Gracie behind."

Marie replied, "What a sad story."

"That's not all." Isabella turned the page and continued, "It says that her ghost has been seen wearing a white dress playing in Johnson Square, which is where her father worked at the Pulaski Hotel. Marie, this fits my vision and is the little girl who came to me pleading for help."

"What kind of help? I wish the visions you two had made more sense." Gale leaned back in the wooden chair and sighed.

"So do we, but that's all we've got."

Gale leaned forward. "Did you get anything from Myra?"

Marie's smile disappeared as she set the book down in front of her. "No, I was wondering why she hasn't come through, but you know she only shows up when I need her or when we're in danger. My spirit guides have been giving me direction, and basically, we've got evil presences in the form of a vampire or not a vampire."

"Oh good, that makes more sense." Gale rolled her eyes and got up from her chair and slid it under the table. "I think I will go find some magazines. I'm having a hard time buying into this stuff, and I'm not much help at the moment."

"That sounds like a good plan." Marie picked up her book again and began to leaf through the pages.

Before Gale could walk away in a huff, Mimi rushed in with her notebook and almost knocked Gale over. "You all will not believe the information I just learned from a woman at the Georgia Historical Society."

Gale stared at Mimi waiting for an apology. "Please, do enlighten us."

"Apparently there is a society of vampires right here in Savannah, and they all follow the code of *The Black Veil*."

Harry asked, "You found that information from the historical society?"

"No, not actually from their records. I met one of the members who is a benefactor, very high up on the food chain if you know what I mean." Mimi plopped herself in Gale's chair and continued, "This woman, Margaret Axelby, was doing some research and we struck up a conversation as to why we were here and what had happened at the Tanners' farm."

"What is the black veil?" Isabella moved closer to Mimi as she intently listened for more information.

"The Black Veil is a guideline for vampires. Margaret met one of the vampires at a local benefit, but apparently learned about this code of so-called ethics for vampires from a friend who had a horrible experience with a vampire."

Gale snorted and sheepishly closed her mouth. "You mean to tell us that there are real vampires here in Savannah?"

"They're all over the world, apparently." Mimi opened her notebook and slid her finger down the page. "There are thirteen guidelines they follow, and one of them is titled, donors. What it states under this item is that feeding should occur between consenting adults. Donors should make informed decisions before they give themselves. They're not to take blood from donors in a greedy fashion. The exchange is to be beneficial to all."

Marie said, "I can't believe there is documentation of vampire ethics. I'd like to learn more from this Margaret."

"Oh, you will, I've invited her along tonight on our investigation. She has a real interest in the paranormal and she said she'd be glad to share her story on this vampire code of ethics."

Harry tried to straighten his bow tie without success and then decided to flatten the wrinkles from his suit coat. "I've heard of there being a society amongst vampires. I've even heard some rumblings of a codebook. I seem to recall there is a House Kheperu that endorsed it."

"That's what Margaret said." Mimi looked at Harry and said, "Harry, how do you know that?"

"How does Harry know anything he knows? He's a walking Wikipedia weirdo." Gale smirked at Harry and then leaned against the shelf of local authors.

"Gale please, this isn't helping." Marie looked back at Harry. "Please continue, Harry. What is this House Kheperu?"

"I believe the meaning is the house of transformation, which would make sense for a vampire. I don't know much else, but I would imagine we can find information."

Isabella swiped through her iPad and said, "Yep, right here it is. They have a Facebook page. It talks about transformation and their spiritual path. They apparently believe in awakening the deeper truths about their nature and the nature of the universe they exist in."

"Spiritual path? How is being a vampire a spiritual path?" Gale pulled yet another chair from a side table and sat down next to Isabella.

Harry replied, "I would imagine it is their spiritual path."

Isabella continued reading out loud. "I think some of this has to do with witchcraft or Wiccan and magic."

Mimi nodded her head. "Yes, Margaret touched on that also."

"All right then, it looks as though we have a great deal of information to take back and share with everyone." Marie looked at her watch. "Mimi, what time did you tell Margaret to meet us at the Tanners?"

"I told her to be there around six thirty. I figured that would give us a little time before we began our investigation, and to fill her in on how we do things. She may be of help to us."

"I agree, so let's pick up some food to take back and get ourselves prepped and ready. I'll text Cory and see how he's made out at the police station. He has a natural ability to make friends."

Gale cinched her ponytail and followed Marie toward the door. "Knowing Cory, they've deputized him, and he's on the case with them."

They all chuckled and made their way to the cars to learn more about vampires and conduct what they do know, which are ghost investigations.

FOUR

MARGARET AXELBY WAS an eccentric looking woman in her mid-to-late sixties with dyed purple hair, cat-eye glasses, and bony hands. She couldn't have weighed more than a hundred pounds and stood only five feet tall. She wore bright flashy clothing and too much expensive jewelry, but she had the warmest smile and a kind face. She was more than willing to help the team, and it was apparent she was thrilled to be a part of the ghost investigation.

Marie almost tripped over Bailey as she adjusted the camera angle in the corner of the barn and tried to focus on the eccentric woman's rambling conversation about her rich family history. "Mrs. Axelby..."

Margaret's southern drawl reply made you feel as though you should be sipping a mint julep and fanning yourself from the heat as the sweat beaded down your cleavage. "Oh please, call me Margaret. Nobody calls me Mrs. Axelby except for my maid, Anna Belle. Even after I've repeatedly asked her not to, she just can't bring herself to call me by my first name."

"Very well, Margaret. Mimi stated that you know something about what is called the Black Veil code amongst vampires. Is this true, and how did it come up as something for you to learn about?"

"Oh my heavens, there has been a dark element in Savannah about vampires that dates back as far as history goes. I remember hearing stories as a child, but there were those who swore up and down they had witnessed vampires slithering around in the dead of night preying on those who were vulnerable." She shifted herself on the bale of hay and continued, "My daddy said that one of the cotton pickers that worked on my great granddaddy's cotton farm had been bit by a vampire and couldn't work out in the sun during the day. He only liked to work at night. They said he had scary red bloodshot eyes, but my daddy would just laugh at the story and said he was probably a drunk and too lazy to work during the day."

"Why did you decide to learn about the Black Veil?"

"My friend Abigail said she had an encounter with one of her lovers who was a vampire. He talked about this code of rules they had to follow and that he couldn't make her a donor unless she freely offered it to him."

Marie stopped short and almost knocked over the camera. "What did she do?"

Margaret let out a hearty laugh. "She hightailed it right out of his house and ran all the way home. She was scared to death. After that, she began to do some research on this code, and she shared it with me. You can find it out on the Internet. That was quite a few years ago, and I've since forgotten about it until Mimi asked me earlier today."

"I'm sure one of my colleagues has already searched for it. We'll have to review it together and see what we're dealing with." Marie finished the camera adjustments and stood next to Margaret. "Why don't we head back to the house? We've secured the kitchen as our headquarters. We can continue our discussion there."

"That sounds fine, and again, I'd like to thank you for including me in this. I find the paranormal fascinating."

The two women and Bailey made their way back to the house where the rest of the team had congregated in the kitchen after finalizing positions on all of the cameras, recorders, and a laser grid. She was glad to hear that Cory had received a friendly welcome from the local police and that they will stay in touch with him if anything else should occur.

As she stepped into the kitchen, she spotted Gale sipping a small glass that contained the homemade Chatham Artillery Punch. Harry was nervously waiting for the investigation to begin as he sat in a chair all alone against the wall. Tim and Cory were enjoying some red velvet cupcakes, while Jim and Mimi were having their usual disagreement over something, and Isabella was feverishly reading something on her iPad.

Marie stepped over beside Isabella and asked, "Hey there, what are you reading?"

Isabella replied without taking her eyes off the screen. "I found a website that lists the thirteen rules of the Black Veil."

"I told Margaret that someone from our team had probably already found this information on the Internet. Before you tell me anything, let me get everyone's attention first, then you can share what you've learned."

"Listen up everyone. Margaret shared some stories with me about how she came to learn about the Black Veil. Isabella has found some information about it on the Internet, and I want her to share it with us. Once she's finished with that, we'll need to get into our investigation." Marie smiled at Isabella. "Go ahead, Isabella. You now have the floor."

Isabella smiled and looked at everyone, and then placed her attention back on the iPad screen and began to read the rules of the vampire community. "Okay, it's a bit lengthy, so I'll try to summarize each of the thirteen rules. It comes from a website that's supposed to be for real vampires."

Harry said, "I believe there were some disagreements amongst these so-called vampires. They eventually rewrote the thirteen rules. Is that what you've learned?"

"Yes, that's what it says." Isabella smiled and continued, "Okay, so here's what the thirteen rules are, the first one is *discretion*, which states that the lifestyle is private and sacred and that they're to respect it as such. It says that someday the world may be ready for them to reveal themselves, but that time is not now. They're not supposed to hide from their nature, but never show it off to those who won't understand.

The second one is *diversity*, and they're essentially on the same journey and they don't all have the answers to who and what they are and the need to remain unified. The third one is *safety*, which says they're to use sense when indulging their nature. They're to feed in private and make sure their donors are discrete. They're supposed to screen their donors carefully and make certain they are in good health both mentally and physically."

Gale finished her punch and shook her head. "I can't believe this crap is out there as a guidebook for vampires."

Isabella replied, "Apparently it is. Number four is *control*. They're not supposed to deny the darkness within them but not let it control them either. If they do, it could cloud their judgment, and they're not supposed to indulge in pointless violence. They're not supposed to feed for the sake of feeding, and never give over to mindless bloodlust. They state that they're not monsters."

Tim rolled his eyes and laughed. "Yeah right, vampires aren't monsters. Who are they kidding?"

Isabella continued, "Number five is *lifestyle*. It says they're privileged to be what they are, but power is to be accompanied by responsibility and dignity. They're to remember that they may be vampires and are still a part of this world, and they must live like everyone else by holding jobs, keeping homes, and getting along with their neighbors.

Six is *family*. They're to respect the greater community when having disputes. Settle their differences quietly amongst each other, and never bring their arguments into public places or force family members to take sides.

Number seven is *havens*, which are private areas where they go to socialize. They're supposed to respect patrons in public places that don't understand their ways. They're not to initiate violence in a haven or bring anything illegal into a haven. It's supposed to be the hub of their whole community, and they should respect it so that they can always call it home."

"Wow, I had no idea this was a thing." Mimi finished eating a piece of cheese and took a sip of water.

Margaret said, "Trust me, that's what Abigail and I thought when we read about this. It was so outrageous to think that people believed they were vampires and that they had a community of bloodsuckers."

Isabella waited for everyone to finish discussing the matter and continued with the final six rules. "Okay, number eight is *territory*. Apparently, there are different cities, and they each have their hierarchy of rules. They're supposed to learn and respect each of these cities. Number nine is *responsibility*. It says the lifestyle isn't for everyone. They're not to bring in anyone who is mentally or emotionally unstable, and they're supposed to teach them control and discretion, and make certain that they respect their ways.

Ten is *elders*, and that's about giving the respect to elders or leaders. It says they're to appreciate the elders for all they have given them, and because of their dedication, the community would not exist.

Number eleven creeps me out. It's titled, *donors*. It says that without those who offer themselves body and soul to them, they would be nothing and the donors sustain their nature. They're not to mistreat their donors, physically or emotionally, nor manipulate or leech off for more than what they freely offer. They're not supposed to take the donors for granted. They should appreciate them for the companionship and acceptance they provide, which so many others would refuse."

Jim shuddered and said, "Okay, that is creepy. Why would a donor freely donate their life to a vampire?"

"I remember in the movie Bram Stoker's Dracula that Winona Ryder gave herself freely. Of course, she was seduced and in a trance." Gale chuckled and poured herself another drink.

Marie raised her right eyebrow at Gale. "You've had enough punch, and that was a movie. These are codes of ethics for vampires. Isabella, can you quickly summarize the last two rules? We need to start our investigation."

"Sure, number twelve is *leadership*, and it states the usual bit about being a good leader, and thirteen is *ideals*, which says that being a vampire isn't just about feeding upon life. It's what they do, but it's not what they are. Representing their darkness in a world blinded by light and accepting their differences, which makes them unique. They're to live without guilt and shame, etcetera, etcetera." Isabella turned off her iPad and closed the case.

Cory looked around the room at everyone's blank stares as he broke the silence. "Wow okay, I don't know about you all, but I'm ready for something normal like a ghost investigation."

Everyone laughed, appreciated the much-needed humor, broke into teams, and went about their routines of the investigation. Jim, Tim, and Harry took their EVP recorders and made their way into the barn as they stood to the side of the laser grid. Cory chose to investigate just outside the barn. Mimi, Margaret, and Gale were in the living room where there had been footsteps and voices heard. Marie, Isabella, and Bailey stayed in the kitchen monitoring the different camera views on their main screen.

Isabella rubbed Bailey's neck and carefully

watched camera four of the barn. "Marie, why do you think Myra hasn't shown up lately?"

"I don't know. Myra is probably busy on the other side. Her natural state is to help others. She's probably doing more than she ever did here." Marie smiled at the memory of her teacher.

"I know you two were close. How did you handle Myra's death at the hands of a demon? I didn't think that was ever possible."

Marie sighed, "Neither did I Isabella...neither did I."

They were instantly interrupted by Bailey's low growl as he stared into the living room. Marie put her attention to camera three where Gale and Mimi were sitting on the living room couch doing an EVP session.

Gale asked, "Is there anyone here with us tonight? Are there any spirits who have seen vampires?"

Mimi giggled but stopped when a noise came from the corner of the room behind her. "What was that? Is there anyone here? Can you tell us your name? The Tanners lost their pig, do you know anything about that?"

Isabella heard Mimi's question from the kitchen and whispered to Marie, "I just saw Gracie. I think she's in the living room right behind Mimi."

Marie kept her eyes on the screen. "I see her too. Are you able to communicate with her?"

"No, she just seems to be wandering frantically behind the couch. She's not making any sense. She looks frightened." Isabella tried to settle Bailey down as she got up from the chair and stood off to the side of the doorway.

"I feel some frigid air right on my back," Gale

yelled into the kitchen. "Marie, are you getting anything on camera?"

"Not on screen, but Isabella and I have seen a presence of Gracie. She looks to be in a panic behind you two."

Gale casually turned around and looked into thin air. "Gracie if that's you, is there anything we can do for you? Don't be afraid. We're here to help the Tanners."

Isabella spoke into the living room. "She's gone, wow that was strange. I wonder why she was here?"

"Let's hope they caught something on their recorders." Marie saw something in her peripheral vision and shifted her attention back to the barn. "I think she's in the barn. Isabella, can you please come in here and take a look at camera four?"

Isabella stepped over Bailey and sat down in the chair as she viewed the laser grid changing shape. "I see it. I think Gracie's in the barn."

Within a few seconds, Tim's voice came over the radio. "Marie, are you catching this on the monitor? It looks to be a small spirit walking through the laser grid."

"Yes, Tim, we see it. Isabella and I think it's the spirit of Gracie. She was just here in the living room. I think she's trying to send a warning. We can't quite make it out."

Cory's voice came on the radio next. "The geopod is going off like crazy, and I'm hearing a very strange low growl coming from behind the barn. I've got my recorder on, so I hope I'm able to capture something."

"There sure is a lot of activity taking place all of a sudden around the barn." Isabella looked at Marie. "Do you think that's a coincidence?"

"Nope, I don't believe in coincidences. I think Gracie was trying to warn us that something was out at the barn, that's why she disappeared from in here so fast." Marie picked up the radio and spoke. "I'm documenting the times when these experiences took place. Make sure all of the recording devices are on. I suspect we're going to have a lot of great evidence from all of this."

Cory replied, "If you want, Tim and I can get the equipment ready to test the spirit box out here. I think it may give us a little more to go on."

"I think that's a great idea. The spirit box and a set of headphones are in here. I'll send Isabella out with them, and you can both try it just outside the barn." Marie stepped down from the stool and found the spirit box and an extra set of headphones. "Isabella, can you please take these out to Cory and Tim?"

"Sure, I haven't seen how this works. Can I stay and watch how the spirit box works?"

"Take this notebook out with you and help Tim write down the responses Cory gives. Tell Cory to plug the headphones into the spirit box. Tim will ask a series of questions, you can help with questions also, and as Cory says words that he hears coming through the spirit box, you can write them down. Be sure to correlate them with the questions you are asking because Cory won't have any idea what you're saying."

Isabella grabbed the equipment, notebook, and pen, and ran for the door. "This should be cool."

Marie looked at Gale as she entered the kitchen and chuckled. "It's fun watching her learn about everything we're doing on these investigations. I wish I had someone to guide me when I was her age."

Gale smiled and said, "Yeah, but don't think of that, just think of what you're able to do for her. As you always say, it's a part of your journey."

Marie scrunched her nose. "I hate it when you throw back my words at me, but apparently you were listening, which is rare."

Gale adjusted the volume on the laptop. "Whatever..."

Marie smiled and looked at the camera screen of Cory adjusting the headphones on his head as Tim and Isabella got situated and ready with their questions. "This should be an interesting test."

Gale spoke into the radio. "Tim, is everyone ready?"

Tim raised his thumb and nodded. "We're ready with our questions. Isabella and I are going to take turns. Once Cory is settled in, we'll begin."

Gale pushed the button on the radio. "Let's roll."

Marie leaned in toward the monitor so she could keep an eye out for any activity that may take place on screen. Even though she enjoyed watching Isabella learn about the paranormal, she also wanted to keep an eye on her.

Tim's voice came through loud and clear on the radio as he asked, "Was that you that was growling a little while ago?"

Cory remained silent with his eyes closed and then said, "Yes."

Isabella's eyes grew large as she looked at Tim and said, "Who are you and are you the one who frightened Elizabeth?"

Cory replied, "Carmilla. No."

Tim continued, "What do you want Carmilla?"

Cory answered, "Eternal life."

Isabella shivered as she rubbed her arms trying to clear the goosebumps. "Are you a vampire?"

Cory remained silent for a few seconds and then said, "Yes...Karnstein...Mircalla."

Tim's eyebrows drew together as he looked at Isabella and shrugged his shoulders. "What do Karnstein and Mircalla mean?"

Cory said, "Ancestors...beast...death."

Before Isabella could ask another question, Cory jumped up and immediately threw off the headphones and looked like a madman with terror in his eyes. "I just heard the most horrific combined low growl and laughter. Holy shit did that send a shiver down my back."

Isabella asked, "Are you okay?"

Cory leaned over and took in a deep breath. "I think so. Did any of what I said make sense?"

Tim replied, "Yes for a couple of questions and not sure on the others. Do you need to take a break? We can head back to the kitchen and share this with Marie. You look like you could use a drink."

"Yeah, I think that's a good idea, but maybe something a little stronger than water." Cory picked up the equipment and followed Isabella and Tim to the kitchen.

They met Marie and Gale on the porch as Marie handed Cory a water bottle. "What the hell just happened? I was following along as much as I could when I saw you shoot up as if you got stabbed in the back. Are you okay?"

Cory chugged down the water and wiped the excess from his mouth with the back of his hand. "Things were going along well until I heard the most sinister growl. It freaked me out. It was very unnerving."

Tim said, "We got some good responses to our questions. I'm not sure about the growl and laugh he heard. It came right after Cory said the words, ancestors, beast, and death. Not sure what any of it means."

"Let's go inside, and you can tell us what happened. Then maybe you and Tim can man headquarters while Isabella, Gale, and I head out to the barn. It's probably time for the group to switch locations."

They took down notes from Cory's experience and continued their investigation until two in the morning. After a long and grueling night, they decided to wrap up everything and head back to the carriage houses. The team members had their separate way to decompress after an investigation, which dictated who bunked in with whom.

Marie, Cory, Gale, Tim, and Isabella shared the larger of the two carriage houses because they usually went to bed first after a long night of investigating. Marie and Isabella would do a cleansing meditation, which helped them to sleep in a more relaxed state to keep their visions down to a minimum. Cory usually read for a short time before turning in. Gale and Tim, on the other hand, had their usual bedroom routine to help them fall asleep.

Harry liked to watch television to unwind, while Mimi and Jim would fry up eggs and bacon, although Mimi had switched to egg whites and turkey bacon with her new diet. They were the night owls of the group and rarely helped with the first round of analysis. Whatever the scenario was for each of them to relax, it helped everyone to keep from getting on each other's nerves.

FIVE

IT WAS standard practice for everyone to meet at eleven a.m. for brunch and they chose to eat outside on the joint brick patio connecting the two carriage houses, which extended from one place to the other with water features embedded into the brick walls. There were crape myrtles, southern magnolia trees, beech trees, and Palmetto palm trees.

The buildings were nestled together between two parallel streets in the heart of the historic district of Savannah, which reminded Marie of New Orleans and Charleston combined. There were colorful historic homes with grand double-decker porches, as well as quaint residences with simple symmetrical square facades. The sidewalks extended in front of each house were lined with live oaks covered in moss, which gave a visitor a cozy welcome to the neighborhood.

The sun was warm, and the birds were in perfect tune as the team gradually arrived one-by-one at the table filled with food from Goose Feather's Cafe, which consisted of bagels and cream cheese, croissants, muffins, fresh fruit, organic yogurt, granola, sticky buns, preserves, coffee, and tea.

Marie's flaxen hair fell on her shoulders covering the sleeves of her bright pink tank top. She tried to adjust the string of her linen Bermuda shorts as she poured a cup of coffee and added cream. The aroma slipped into her nostrils and brought a sense of calm to her. She quickly snatched some fruit and yogurt and smiled at Cory heading her way. "Good morning husband, I tried to be as quiet as I could organizing this smorgasbord."

Cory's V-neck navy shirt hugged his muscled torso, while his gray jersey gym shorts draped nicely against his firm buttocks and thighs. He leaned over and kissed her on the forehead. "You didn't wake me, the coffee did. This food looks great. When did it arrive?"

"It came about fifteen minutes ago. Look at how huge those strawberries are."

"I'm gonna have one of these bagels and cream cheese." Cory grabbed an onion bagel and poured a cup of coffee.

Eventually, the entire group had arrived, and they ate their way through brunch devouring every morsel of food and sat around finishing their drinks and discussing how the investigation went.

Gale closed her eyes as a smile fell on her face while she sipped her coffee. Her auburn hair was piled up high in a loose bun exposing her bronze skin under her banana yellow chiffon shirt. She casually draped her legs onto Tim's lap as her caramel silk pajama pants nestled against his thighs. "I've got to hand it to you, Marie. This is one of the best brunches we've had on an investigation."

"I'll have to agree with that statement." Jim held his coffee cup up and saluted Marie as his Carolina Panthers baseball hat shaded his eyes from the sun. He looked scrawny under his white cotton T-shirt and royal blue sweatpants.

Mimi shifted her glasses up her nose and gently wiped her sweaty brow with a napkin. The heat had caused the sweat to protrude onto her green cotton pajamas. "Thank you for ordering more fruit. It keeps me away from those scrumptious looking muffins over there."

Marie smiled. "You're very welcome."

Isabella popped another piece of bran muffin into her mouth and gulped down milk as she wiped the excess from her chin. She wore a Beauty and the Beast T-shirt with powder blue cotton sweatpants. "Are we ready to discuss our experiences from last night?"

Harry rolled the sleeves of his cotton, long-sleeved white dress shirt up to his elbows and took a sip of water. His khaki pants were rumpled and bore a strange looking stain at the knee. "I agree. We have a lot of audio and video to review for the Tanners."

Cory said, "I'd just like to say that my experience with the spirit box was one I'll never forget. That sinister laugh gave me nightmares. Has anyone figured out who Carmilla is?"

"I think I did." Isabella flipped open her iPad and began to scroll on the screen. "Carmilla is a vampire and a work of fiction that was written by Joseph Sheridan Le Fanu in eighteen seventy-two. It predates Bram Stoker's, Dracula, by twenty-five years."

"Okay, so how does a supposed work of fiction relate to what Cory experienced? You can't tell me that there's an actual vampire by the name of Carmilla going on a pig killing spree." Gale set her cup down on the table and wiggled her feet in Tim's lap indicating a plea for a foot rub.

"I don't know, but I downloaded the book and briefly read the first chapter before I fell asleep. There was even a series done on YouTube in Canada. I'd like to read more about it so we can better understand if the Carmilla that Cory mentioned last night is the same vampire."

Marie put her coffee cup on the empty bench and leaned forward in her chair. "I think that would be a great idea, Isabella. We all know there are no coincidences. I can't wrap my head around there being vampires either, but we do need to learn more about this story. I have a sneaky feeling this is going to tie together with our investigation."

"Maybe I can call Margaret to let me into the historical societies library. She may be able to help me find any events that may have taken place here back in eighteen seventy-two." Mimi got up from her chair and made her way back to the carriage house.

Gale asked, "By the way, Margaret got quiet after Cory's episode in the barn. Do you think she got freaked out?"

"It's possible. Not everybody can handle what we do." Marie looked at Harry. "What's on your mind, Harry? You're looking very pensive."

"Maybe the rest of us can start making our way through our recordings. We promised Mrs. Tanner that we'd have something for her before they went on vacation at the end of the week."

"Harry's right, we'll need to make that a priority. Isabella, can you put reading that story on the back burner for now? We'll need extra eyes and ears for our analysis." Marie looked at Cory. "Do you think you may be able to get a little more information from the local police? You said you got a nice reception chatting with them yesterday."

Cory winked and said, "I'll try my best."

Marie smiled and returned the wink. "All right, let's clean up this mess first, and then we can set up our equipment out here. We should have enough room. We'll get as much done today as we can and see if we can set up a meeting with the Tanners tomorrow morning."

Everyone dispersed into action while Marie felt a shiver run down her spine, which usually meant there was some activity going to take place on the horizon.

The moon's glow illuminated the bedroom as his mouth lingered at the nape of her creamy neck. He took in the scent of her blood as the beat of her heart hammered in his ears. She was a beautiful woman at the tender age of twenty-three, and she anxiously waited for his tender kiss. He had baited her for months until she finally gave him permission for his seduction. She was an easy donor with many insecurities, which he carefully distinguished one-by-one, telling her she had no reason to fear him or anyone else who relished in her beauty.

He lifted her mesmerized listless body further up the pillow as he whispered in Romanian into her ear. "Lasă-mă hrănesc cu sânge și vă voi da viața veșnică."

She replied in a frenzy of lust and impatience, "Yes, give me eternal life. Take my blood and make me a part of you."

His grin faded, and he quickly bit into her neck as her body quivered in pain and then fell silent and lifeless beneath him. He continued to feed hungrily as the vessels in his body began to dance in an ecstatic heated rapture. He sated his hunger and slowly finished draining the last bit of blood as he licked the wound and then kissed her forehead.

He wiped his mouth with the back of his hand and whispered one last time in her ear. "Rest my child, and I will visit again when both our desires need to be met."

He carefully shifted her body on the bed and swiftly descended the stairs and made his way outside into the waiting black sedan. He met the driver's eyes staring back at him from the rearview mirror and nodded. The car sped off as he dropped his head back on the seat and thought, yes, he will sleep well tonight, as his lips formed a small smile and a low chuckle rose from his throat.

THE SIPS TEAM arrived at the Tanners after lunch the next day for the reveal as they carefully shared their findings. Marie asked Harry to take the lead as she explained in detail what the team felt were the reasons behind their results. She normally wouldn't speak of her psychic ability until she felt the client would be receptive to that side of the paranormal.

When Harry came to the section of the recording where Isabella and Marie saw the spirit of Gracie, she carefully watched their response and said, "I'm sure you're wondering how Isabella and I were able to discern who the spirit was. If you are open to it, we'd like to share with you a little background on what we're able to do."

The Tanners all nodded their heads as Marie explained about her and Isabella's abilities and how each of them can help on an investigation. Marie described how they could see, hear, and speak with spirits on the other side of the veil as well as Marie's psychometry ability to touch things and get pictures of energy residue from certain objects. The Tanners seemed receptive, and Marie felt quite comfortable sharing this information.

After a lengthy conversation, Marie asked, "Does any of this make any sense for you?"

Elizabeth replied, "Yes, it does. We've heard many stories of folks around town seeing the spirit of Gracie. Some of my friend's parents saw her, and none of them are crazy."

Marie smiled, "I'm glad you feel that way. It's a hard thing to share and explain to people who aren't as open as all of you."

"But how does any of this explain what happened to our pig and what Elizabeth saw in the barn?" Barbara Tanner rubbed her shoulders as if to ward off a chill.

"Unfortunately, we're not quite sure we have the answers to that yet. It takes some time to tie everything together, but we did have some activity on that front when my husband, Cory, experienced a few things on our spirit box. We weren't going to reveal any of it because it's speculation at this point, but if you're open to it, we can share that with you now." Marie shifted the laptop from Harry and began to search for the captured voices from that exact moment.

Harry handed each of them a set of earphones as they intently watched the screen and listened to the recording of Cory, Tim, and Isabella asking questions and receiving answers from the spirit box. All three of them jumped when the recording hit the evil growl and chuckle. Marie glanced at Gale with wide eyes and then placed her attention back to the Tanners as they removed their earphones.

"I'm sure that's a little unsettling. It was for my husband too. We're not sure how any of this ties in with what took place in your barn, but I can promise you we will find the answers." Marie closed the laptop and waited for a response.

"Who is Carmilla?" Elizabeth's color slowly came back to her face as she leaned back in the kitchen chair.

Isabella was about to speak when Marie touched her arm and said, "We're not quite sure. Mimi, one of our members and historian, is looking into that." Marie gave Isabella a warm smile and continued, "We plan on staying here a few more days. Cory is at the police station now trying to see if there were any other types of slaughtering's in the area that match what happened to your pig. As we learn more, we will keep you apprised of anything that can shed some light on what happened here."

Barbara smiled and slowly stood up from her chair and said, "Thank you. Thank you all for coming here and helping us out. You've shed some light on a few things, and your compassion has eased our minds. Now let me give you a box of my famous pink lemonade cookies. You'll just love the lemon and hint of raspberry flavor."

Gale frowned and muttered under her breath, "I was hoping for a thermos of her spiked punch."

Isabella giggled and then anxiously waited for Barbara to return from the pantry. "I love these cookies."

The team said their goodbyes and snagged some cookies out of the box for the ride back to the carriage houses. Marie felt a sense of pride knowing yet again they were able to help another family.

Isabella shoved a piece of an iced pink lemonade cookie in her mouth and said, "Marie, why wouldn't you let me share what we learned about Carmilla with the Tanners?"

Marie put on the left turn signal and looked in the rearview mirror at Isabella. "Because I'm not sure if we're dealing with a vampire from the eighteen seventies. Plus, that was a little too much information to dump on them right now. We were able to solve a few of their paranormal occurrences, and hopefully, we'll have a reasonable answer for what happened to their pig. Besides, I think Barbara was more concerned that her daughter wasn't losing her mind."

"Yeah, I think Elizabeth was too." Isabella finished the rest of her cookie and chugged down the rest of her water bottle.

Marie pulled into their assigned parking spot on East Taylor Street when her cell phone rang. The formal sounding woman on the Bluetooth stated a call from Cory's cell. Marie hit the button on the steering wheel and said, "Hello there, we just got back from our reveal. What's up?"

"I was hoping you can come and meet me on Tybee Island. While I was here talking to Detective Captain Hayes, she received a call that they found a young woman's body on the beach, and they found two small puncture wounds in her neck."

"Are you serious?" Marie looked over at Gale sitting on the passenger side of their SUV.

Gale asked, "Is anyone else allowed to come?"

Cory replied, "For now, I think it'd be best if only Marie came. I shared Marie's abilities with Tiffany."

"Tiffany, so Detective Captain Tiffany is a woman?" Gale made a *so why is he talking to another woman* face at Marie.

Marie rolled her eyes. "I'll be in about twenty minutes if the traffic is light. I'd like to freshen up a little if that's okay with you."

"That's fine. I'll text you the exact spot of where we'll be. See you in a few."

"Sounds good." Marie disconnected the call and looked at Gale. "What was that comment all about?"

"Why do you have to freshen up?"

"Don't answer my question with another question. I'm not the one who has jealous tendencies." Marie hopped out of the car and came around to the wrought iron gate.

Gale followed Isabella and let out a huff. "I don't have any jealous tendencies. Where'd you get that idea?"

Isabella snorted. "You're the one who is always giving Tim the evil eye when he looks in any direction at another woman."

Gale stopped short and slammed her hands on her hips. "I do not. Since when have I ever done that?"

Marie reached the door of the carriage house and began entering the code into the keypad. "Look I don't have time to debate this with you. We all know that you flip out on Tim when any woman is within five feet of him."

Isabella followed Marie inside and said, "Yeah, there was the time we were in the library with that new librarian. And then there was the time we were doing that investigation at the Millers, oh and the time we had that guest speaker at one of our meetings..."

Gale threw her purse on the couch and put up her hand and glared at Isabella. "Okay, I get it, I've had a few moments where I may have gotten a little upset about Tim paying attention to other women."

Marie stuck her head out from the bathroom. "A little upset? Gale, you do need to give Tim a break because he is so wrapped up in love with you, it's pitiful. He only has eyes for you, so relax and quit putting your fears over onto Cory and me. Okay?"

"Yeah okay, I hear you." Gale plopped down onto the couch as Tim walked through the door.

"We stopped and picked up some beer for everyone." Tim looked at Gale's exasperated look as he put the beer in the refrigerator. "Is there something going on?"

Isabella said, "Gale's driving Marie nuts again."

"I see." Tim leaned over the back of the couch and kissed the back of Gale's head.

Marie stepped out of the bathroom and slipped into a pair of flip-flops. "As for me, I'm meeting Cory on Tybee Island. He just called and said they found a young woman's body on the beach with two small puncture wounds in her neck."

"You're kidding me. You don't think the woman got bit by a vampire, do you?" Tim sat down next to

Gale, wrapped his arm around her, and pulled her close.

"I'm not sure, but that's why he wants me there, maybe to see if I can pick up on anything. He said he explained my psychic abilities with the detective he met at the police station. She must have been receptive; otherwise, I wouldn't be joining him."

Isabella turned on the television and glanced over at Tim. "Which is why Gale is driving Marie nuts because this detective is a woman and Gale made it sound like Cory was flirting with her."

"I see, well I'm sure Gale was just kidding, right?" Tim tweaked the tip of Gale's nose.

"I can speak for myself. You don't need to talk as if I'm not here." Gale stuck out her tongue at Isabella and snuggled her head into Tim's shoulder.

Marie grabbed her purse and walked toward the door. "As sweet as this is, I need to head out. I'll keep you posted. I'm sure we'll be back in time for some dinner. Isabella, keep an eye on these two, heaven knows they need supervision."

Isabella giggled as she ducked out of the path of a flying pillow from Gale. "You can count on me."

SIX

Tybee Island was a parallel island to Savannah and consisted of a small town with shops, restaurants, and wide sandy beaches hosting a pier and pavilion. There was an eighteenth-century lighthouse that still functioned and a museum that focused on the local history.

Marie spotted Cory standing next to a tall, middle-aged woman with gray hair wearing a uniform as she muttered to herself, "Looks like Gale was wrong."

Cory turned his head and said, "Marie, this is Detective Captain Tiffany Hayes." He glanced at the Captain and continued, "Captain Hayes, this is my wife, Marie. I'd like her to see if she can get a feel for anything from the crime scene, if that's okay."

Marie extended her hand to the Captain with a smile. "So nice to meet you and thank you for allowing me to come. There aren't a lot of people who agree with this kind of thing."

"Not a problem, and please call me Tiffany. Cory explained to me about your psychic abilities, and I'm more than intrigued."

Marie released Tiffany's hand and replied, "What exactly did you find?"

Tiffany pointed to the edge of the crime scene tape where a group of individuals stooped over a young female body. "From what we've surmised, our victim is a white female, approximately in her early twenties, and we believe someone dumped her body here. The only wound found were two small punctures on the side of her neck. There was no blood, which is why we suspect the murder took place somewhere else. The medical examiner will be able to give us a better report once he's done an autopsy. We're still checking in to see who she is. She didn't have a purse or any identification."

"I see." Marie looked at Cory. "What is it you'd like me to do?"

"Do you think you can get a sense of what may have happened? You won't be able to go near the body, but I thought you might be able to sense something from the crime scene."

"I'll see what I can do. Do you have anything of hers that I may be able to touch?"

Tiffany grabbed a pair of sandals in an evidence bag from one of the officers and handed it to Marie. "Will this work?"

"Yes, this will be perfect."

Marie held the bagged sandals in her hands and closed her eyes. The waves of the ocean sent her into a hypnotic state as she tried to summon her spirit guides. Within a few seconds, she began to see pictures flash in front of her.

She saw the young woman laughing and drinking at what looked like a party. Then the girl was dancing with a man, but Marie couldn't see his face. She kept willing for him to turn around, but it was almost as if the man sensed Marie was watching them.

The next thing she saw was a dark room with lit candles and a grand four-poster bed. Marie sensed the girl was nervous, but she smiled at the gentleman as he leaned over and began to kiss her neck.

Marie could hear the deafening sound of the girl's heart beating loudly in her ears. It was almost too loud for Marie to stand and before she could see what happened next, she felt water on her legs and then a hand touched her shoulder. Her eyes opened to see Cory's face blocking the sun from her face. The ocean waves splashed against her skin as she shifted to her knees.

"Are you okay?" Cory pulled Marie up off the sand into a standing position.

"Yes, I'm fine. As per usual, I had a snippet of scenes of this young girl, but it's always difficult to make sense of them."

Tiffany's right eyebrow rose as she shaded the sun from her eyes. "That was one of the strangest things I've ever seen. What exactly happened to you?"

Marie took the bottle of water Cory handed her and gulped half of it down. She returned the cap and wiped her mouth. "What I just used when I touched the shoes is called psychometry. I'm able to feel any energy residue left on an object, and it will give me pictures of the person or people who handled the object. In this case, her shoes."

Cory rubbed Marie's shoulder. "What were you able to see?"

"I saw this girl at some party drinking and dancing with a man. I couldn't see his face. In fact, I tried to will him to turn around and it was almost as if he knew I was watching him in this scene. It was very odd. Then I saw the two of them in a bedroom lit with candles, and I could sense how nervous she was, but also excited at the same time. Then he began kissing her neck and then everything went dark."

Tiffany said, "Were you able to pick up on where this party may have been? Say things that were in the room?"

"Yes, I saw many chandeliers and some ornate architectural circles on the ceiling, which is odd. There was a fireplace in the room where I saw the bed, but that's all I can remember right now. I may remember more later, but as I said, these are snippets, and at times they don't make much sense."

"But they always lead up to answers eventually. It's never failed us to this point." Cory winked and then smiled at Marie.

"Right, well I thank you, Marie, for coming out and sharing your gift. If there's anything else that comes up from your vision, let me know. In the meantime, I'm going to see what more we can learn from the autopsy." Tiffany turned to Cory and extended her hand. "Thanks again Cory and I'll keep you posted on the findings."

Cory shook Tiffany's hand and nodded. "I appreciate that."

Marie smiled and turned to walk with Cory back to their vehicle. "Do you think she believed anything I told her?"

"Hard to say. I've always told you I like the hard facts. That's how cops are wired, but Tiffany wouldn't have asked you here, otherwise."

"I get it. The vision I saw was a bit muddled. I'm not quite sure what it all meant. The thing that struck me odd was that it felt as though the gentleman in the vision was trying to keep his face from being seen. It's as if he was present at that moment in my vision. Almost as if he knew I was trying to see his face. It was creepy. I got the feeling he was manipulating my vision. I've never had that happen before." Marie handed the keys to Cory and got on the passenger side of the SUV. She grabbed a towel from the backseat and dried the ocean water from her legs.

"Is that even possible?" Cory started the engine and backed out of the parking lot.

"I don't know, but I think I need to learn a little more about the abilities of vampires. I remember reading or hearing somewhere that they can put their victims in a trance. I guess I need to stop passing vampires off as a myth and take it a little more seriously. I think Isabella will be able to help me on this one."

Cory replied, "Before I bring any of this to Captain Hayes, I'd like to have more concrete facts regarding this theory. It's hard enough explaining your psychic abilities, let alone vampires running rampant in Savannah."

Marie leaned over and kissed Cory's cheek. "I appreciate you telling her and including me. It means a lot."

"That's what I do. Happy wife, happy life."

Her coal black mussed hair draped over her shoulders and down her back as the sheer lace black veil cast a shadow against her pale gray face. Her black taffeta dress touched the floor and was bustled high at the back, while the bodice boasted a flat front with tiny black glass buttons cascading down from her neck to her abdomen.

She gave a lazy smile and glared her red hollow eyes at Serafino. "So you believe there was a psychic that entered your mind?"

Serafino took a sip of blood and then set the silver chalice on a marble side table. "She didn't enter my mind, but the memory of one of my donors, which I had planned on using for future endeavors until they found the body on Tybee Island. Someone disposed of her body."

"So you were careless? Not only did you lose a donor, but you also let a psychic learn of what took place? It sounds as though you have a traitor amongst your house. Have you learned who it may be?" Carmilla glided along the top of the concrete floor and stopped directly in front of Serafino.

"I'm looking into the matter. I shall take care of the situation. You needn't worry yourself."

With the flash of her hand, she lifted Serafino up and threw him against the wall with such force it knocked the air out of him as he dropped like a limp rag doll to the floor. He tried to remain in his disguised shapeshifted identity as she swiftly moved next to him and lifted his head up to her lips.

"I suggest you take care of this matter expeditiously, so I do not have to step in and take care of it myself. You also need to take care of this psychic. I've dealt with these mystics over the centuries, and I've seen them destroy many covens. I'll not let this be the cause of my extinction." She abruptly dropped his head onto the concrete and vaporized.

Serafino slowly sat up and shouted at the top of his lungs. "Bring me Nicolai!"

. . .

Marie and Cory filled the SIPS team in on the body found on Tybee Island and what took place in Marie's vision. The team sat around the living room and concurred that it was odd for the gentleman in her vision to keep his face from being exposed.

Isabella swiftly turned on her iPad and began typing on the attached keyboard. "Look, the same thing happened in the Vampire Diaries series. Vampires were able to use telepathy to read and control the minds of their victims. It's a known fact throughout vampire folklore. I think it's completely possible that the gentleman in your vision was a vampire and he knew you were seeing what took place in his victim's mind. It makes sense that he wouldn't allow you to see his face."

"This is completely ridiculous. Come on people, do you seriously believe we're dealing with vampires? I know Marie's abilities are real, but this just seems a little far-fetched to me." Gale chuckled and sat down in the plush brown suede love seat.

Harry slid his glasses up the bridge of his nose and wiped his brow with his wrinkled handkerchief. "We can't rule any of this out. I say we tread lightly, and I agree with Marie, we need to learn more about the abilities and characteristics of vampires."

Mimi's cell phone rang as she tapped the screen and walked into the kitchen to better hear her caller. After a few minutes, she hung up and returned to the group. "That was Margaret. She just invited us to a masquerade ball being hosted by the historical society this evening at The Olde Pink House. She knows it's late notice, but she said that there's a strong possibility the vampire community will be there. She also wants us to meet someone who has a huge wealth of knowledge on vampires. Apparently, he has been doing quite a bit of investigating here. I believe she said his name was General Spielsdorf."

Tim asked, "A general, what branch of service?"

"I have no idea, but he may be a good source to learn more about vampires and what's taking place here in Savannah."

Isabella began to hurriedly search on her iPad and said, "Did you get the first name of this general?"

"Yes, I think she said, Baron."

"Oh my, it can't be. I don't believe it." Isabella turned to her iPad and began reading and then looked back at the group. "Do you all remember me telling you about the story of the vampire Carmilla?" After seeing their nods she continued, "Well the one guy in the story who was tracking her is named General Baron Spielsdorf."

Jim sat straight up in his chair and looked at everyone. "Are you serious? I don't think that's a coincidence."

"No, we all know our feelings on that subject. It looks like there's another layer to this case. I think we need to be at this ball. But first I'll need to check with the owner of these carriage houses to see if we can add some more time to our visit. Is everyone's schedule open?" Marie grabbed her cell phone and scrolled through her emails to find the owner's contact information.

Once everybody made the needed phone calls back home to extend their stay, they all agreed they needed to rent some costumes for the masquerade ball. Isabella found a novelty shop online as they made their way to Garden City, Georgia.

Marie entered the shop first and noticed the

dresses for the women were classy and luxurious, while the range of styles for the men included tuxedos, silk shirts and vests, and red and black winged-tipped shoes. They found many stylish masks in an array of styles. Some had feathers, while others boasted glitter, satin, lace, and paper-mache. It was obvious that the mask set the tone for the rest of the ensemble.

Gale stepped out of the dressing room wearing a black sequin dress that made her look like Morticia from the Addams family, while her mask was made of black satin and lace and only covered her eyes.

Marie chose a bright blush beaded gown with a scoop neckline and low scoop back with three quarter length sleeves. Her mask was gold with glitter and extended to her upper lip.

Isabella's indigo chiffon dress stopped at her calves while the lace capped sleeves and neckline exposed her tanned skin. She chose a silver mask with sapphire feathers.

Mimi's dress was a purple taffeta that stopped just at her knee with a satin band that rested just under her bosom. Her mask flourished with ribbons and beads that covered her entire face.

The men chose elegant black or grey tuxedos and white shirts, but each selected a mask that fit their personalities. Cory had a half black and white hard plastic mask that ended at the tip of his nose. Tim chose a matte black paper-mache mask that rested on his cheekbones. Jim decided on a red beaded cat eye mask, while Harry selected a full-face court jester style mask.

They took their costumes back to the carriage houses and decided to order take out to give them enough time to get ready for the ball. Marie couldn't bring Bailey along, so she secured a dog sitter for him for the evening. Everyone thought the ball sounded promising for a good time but also knew they could be dealing with vampires.

Marie struggled with the stranger in her vision and why he chose not to reveal his face. She also wondered how a general with the exact name from a story written in the eighteen hundreds could be at this ball. Her biggest fear was exposing Isabella to an unknown situation possibly involving vampires. She worked very hard at protecting her, but she knew how stubborn Isabella could be, along with having a curious nature. Those were two risky traits to have, and she vowed to herself to protect Isabella to the nth degree.

SEVEN

A STRING QUARTET played Vivaldi's Four Seasons Spring as its tune floated from the windows of the pink stucco colonial mansion. As Marie approached closer, she admired the Greek portico and the majestic fanlight that hung over the door. The team ascended the stairs and made their way through the crowd and eventually found the entrance. A jester greeted them while standing on a lovely Georgian stairway.

Guests decorated in luxurious costumes and masks filled the rooms as far as the eye could see. There was laughing, singing, and dancing as waiters wearing grey satin masks maneuvered trays filled with glasses of champagne among the attendees.

Gale carefully grabbed two glasses and handed one to Tim. "These waiters look like the Lone Ranger."

Tim chuckled and took a sip of champagne. "Wow, this is good. By the way, did I tell you how gorgeous you look in that dress?"

Gale savored the bubbly liquid sliding down her

throat and said, "Yes, about twenty times. What's gotten into you tonight?"

"I don't know. I think it's the mask. Maybe you could just leave that on later."

"I'm going to take that as a compliment because one would think you prefer to have my face hidden." Gale drained the last drop from the glass and slipped it on one tray and grabbed another from a waiter heading in the opposite direction.

"You know I adore your face. It's just something mystical about wearing a mask."

"I think that's why they have these balls. People like to pretend to be someone else for an evening." Gale grabbed Tim's hand and guided him over to the table of hors-d'oeuvres. "Come on, I see caviar over there."

Marie made sure Isabella stuck close to her as they struggled to make their way through the groups of people. She spotted couples sneaking up the stairs and kissing in corners of the hallway, and she hoped it wasn't too risqué for Isabella.

"Harry, why don't you take Isabella over to that table and get yourselves something to eat. The food looks amazing."

Harry replied, "I'm not hungry."

"I'd still like you to escort Isabella, please." Marie leaned closer to Harry's ear. "I'd like you to steer her away from that couple groping each other over there. Make sure you keep an eye on her."

Harry glanced over in the direction of Marie's stare and shook his head. "Of course, I'd be glad to."

Marie watched Isabella take Harry's elbow and smiled, and then walked over toward Cory and Mimi and grabbed a glass of champagne along the way. "Mimi, have you seen Mrs. Axelby?"

"No, I haven't. I was just telling Cory she told me she would be wearing a costume representing Marie Antoinette, but honestly, I've seen a dozen women who look like her. I guess we'll have to wait until she finds us."

"Yes, and we'll need to try and stick together. Do you know where Jim is?" Marie finished her glass and set it on a waiter's tray.

Mimi's ribbons and beads danced on her mask when she spoke. "I have no idea, but I wouldn't doubt he's somewhere close to that voluptuous woman wearing what looked like a French maid outfit."

"Oh dear, well I'll keep an eye out for him, and in the meantime, we'll do the same for Mrs. Axelby."

The music came to a stop, and one of the Marie Antoinette's grabbed a microphone and began welcoming everyone to the ball. The voice was Mrs. Axelby, and Marie moved her mask up in a sleuth-like manner to catch her attention. Mrs. Axelby spotted Marie and nodded her head. When she had finished her welcome speech, she set the microphone back in its stand and made her way over to where they were standing.

Margaret meandered her way next to Marie with a handsome gentleman in tow, while Harry and Isabella arrived at the same time. Marie waved her hand in a come-hither gesture at Gale and Tim and then asked Cory to drag Jim away from the voluptuous French maid.

Mrs. Axelby adjusted her white satin mask and leaned in toward Marie. "This damn mask keeps sticking to the perspiration on my face. I declare it's hot in here." She grabbed a glass of champagne and took a sip. "There that's better. Now, before I introduce you to General Spielsdorf, I'd like for you to meet my colleague here at the historical society, Alexander Pride. He's an attorney at Ikeholz Law Firm located on Broad Street."

Alexander's blue-tinted wire-rimmed glasses fell just below the bridge of his nose where his mask began, making it difficult to see his eyes. His hair shimmered like a raven's feathers, and his blinding smile created divots in his cheeks. "Hello, it's nice to meet you."

Margaret said, "We've hosted many events together, and he's shared some fascinating stories about some of the people he's met along the way. He has graciously agreed to chat with us about the vampire community at a later time. He has quite a bit of knowledge and has even met a few vampires."

Isabella asked, "Real vampires?"

Alexander gave Isabella a broad smile and shook his head. "No, they claim to belong to the vampire community, but honestly, I think they just like to pretend they are vampires."

Margaret laughed and ever so slightly touched Alexander's arm. "We can all chat later. For now, let us go and meet the general."

They said their goodbyes while Marie turned to see Cory and Jim were not far behind. As the team made their way to one of the back rooms, Marie glanced in a side room and stopped short, while Gale and Tim slammed right into her back.

Gale said, "What are you doing? Why'd you quit walking? I nearly spilled all of my champagne."

Marie ignored her questions and made her way

into the side room and looked straight up at the ceiling. "This is the room I saw in my vision when I was holding the victim's shoes. I think we're in the same place."

Cory came up behind her and glanced around the empty room filled with unset tables and piles of table linens stacked on a long antique oak credenza. "Are you sure?"

"Yes, the circles on the ceiling match what I saw in my vision. Apparently, the woman was here having dinner before taken to the bedroom. I suspect that room is upstairs also. They have accommodations here."

Isabella and the rest of the team entered the room. "Are you sensing anything?"

Marie looked at Isabella shook her head. "No, I'm not getting anything now, but this is the place."

Mrs. Axelby stuck her head in the door. "There you all are. I turned to introduce you to the general, and you were all gone. Is everything okay?"

"Yes, everything is fine. I'm sorry, I guess I was just curious about this room." Marie turned and shrugged her head to the team to leave and follow Mrs. Axelby. "We're right behind you this time, I promise."

They left the room and walked further down the hall and then made their way downstairs. The air was cooler than the main ballroom and a welcome relief to the warm surroundings from upstairs. They walked a few more feet and stepped into a small room with wine colored brick walls and worn cherry hardwood floors.

There was a fireplace on the main wall, and a round table surrounded by two leather winged back chairs that looked as though you could melt right into the cowhide. At the corner table sat a portly but distinguished gentleman with curly gray hair protruding underneath his black and white tragedy mask, which had been haphazardly resting on the top of his head. He looked as if he was portraying Napoleon as he feverishly scribbled in a notebook.

He hadn't noticed the nine people standing next to a grand piano staring at him. He stopped to take a sip of brandy and spied over the rim of the snifter glass and jumped as he spoke in a genteel British accent. "Oh good heavens, you all startled me." He glanced at Margaret and continued, "Mrs. Axelby, I assume this is the group of individuals you told me about?"

"I just love it when you say my name. Yes, these are the wonderful people from Sullivan's Island, and they are a paranormal group who do ghost investigations." Margaret introduced everyone as the team took a seat close to the general. "I'll leave you all in the general's capable hands. I need to get back to the ball."

"Yes, thank you Mrs. Axelby, and it's nice to meet you all." He pointed to the square glass decanter. "Help yourselves. It's a fifteen-year-old Remy Martin cognac. It soothes the soul."

Gale started toward the decanter when Marie gave her the stink eye warning her off. "Thank you, but no, we've had our fill of champagne." Marie caught Gale's eye roll and continued, "We were hoping to learn some things about vampires. Margaret stated that you knew all there was and that you've been studying them for many years."

Baron gestured his hand for Marie to sit next to

him in the adjoining leather chair and then took another sip of cognac. "Yes, it feels like several lifetimes. My research has brought me to Savannah. There seems to be the possibility of a clan here."

"A clan? You mean like a family?" Isabella scooted her wooden chair closer to Marie.

"Yes, that's right. This clan descends from the matriarch Carmilla."

Gale sat up in her chair and looked at Isabella and then gave her attention to the general. "Did you say Carmilla? That's the name we got on our investigation at the Tanners."

"What do you mean you got the name Carmilla? How did this happen?"

Marie replied, "There are many different types of equipment we use when we investigate where there is paranormal activity. One of the devices is called a spirit box, which uses radio frequencies to speak to the dead. During one of these encounters, my husband Cory mentioned the name Carmilla."

Tim said, "Yeah and shortly after that he heard an awful growl. We have it on a recording."

The general's eyebrows went up as he set his snifter glass down and sat back in his chair. "Is there any way you can allow me to hear this recording?"

Marie replied, "Absolutely, we'd love to talk more with you about all of this. I don't think tonight is a good time to get into a discussion of what you've learned about vampires."

The general heard Gale giggle as he clucked his tongue in her direction. "This isn't anything to laugh about my dear. These beasts are deadly and the more you know how to defend yourself, the better off you'll be. You'll also need to be cautious at the ball. There are likely vampires amongst us, and they'll be looking for their next victims."

Marie nodded at the general and again gave Gale the stink eye. "Yes, I think Gale has had a little too much to drink. Is there a place where we can meet tomorrow?"

"Yes, you can all come back to this room. I'm staying here. Shall we say eight tomorrow morning?"

Marie ignored Gale's groan and said, "That sounds great. We'll bring our evidence with us so you can listen to our findings."

"Very well." The general stood up and took Marie's hand and brushed his lips on her knuckles. "It was nice to meet you all, and I look forward to our meeting tomorrow."

Marie smiled. "Likewise and thank you for your time."

As the team left the room and walked up the stairs, Gale said, "Oooh, I think General Baron has a thing for Marie. Cory, you'd better keep your sword arm free in case you need to defend her honor."

The group laughed as they made their way back to the ballroom to continue in the festivities. Marie tried to enjoy herself, but she couldn't help but wonder who stood behind the many masks, and which of them were vampires.

Serafino stood at the end of the hall and watched them come from the basement and enter the ballroom. He immediately sensed he had found his psychic and watched her make her way onto the dance floor with a gentleman, as they joined in with the others spinning across the floor. In mid-stride, he caught her eyes behind her mask as he tried to read her mind. He carefully watched her from behind a pillar to remain hidden and quickly turned his head and walked over to the other side of the room. He kept his back to her and chuckled as he realized this would be the beginning of an engaging relationship.

Cory felt Marie's back tense as he pulled her close to him. "Are you okay? You seem very stiff all of a sudden. Do you want to stop dancing?"

"No, no I'm fine. I just got the strangest feeling that someone was trying to enter my thoughts."

Cory pulled his head back from her cheek and looked her in the eyes. "Do you think it's the same gentleman you had in your vision?"

"I think so. Before I could figure out which direction it was coming from, it stopped. I sense it was coming from the corner of the room, but now I don't see anyone." Marie swiveled her head around the room as they danced in search of the mysterious person. "I couldn't get a good look at anyone. That was strange. Mrs. Axelby said there would be vampires here. It's impossible to see anyone behind their masks."

Cory guided Marie along the antique floorboards and then eventually maneuvered her off to the side. "Isn't that the whole reason people come to these masquerade balls? It's a chance for them to escape and pretend to be someone else. In their case, they can disguise themselves from being vampires. If indeed we are dealing with vampires."

Marie adjusted her sleeves and grabbed a glass of champagne from one of the many trays being dispersed by waiters. "I can't seem to bring myself to believe any of that either. But I can't deny that was a very odd experience, and it was the same feeling I had in my vision."

Cory spooned caviar onto a cracker and popped it in his mouth. "Do you want to walk around and see if you can find whoever it was?"

"No, I get the sense they're no longer here." Marie dipped a shrimp in the cocktail sauce and took a bite. "These hors-d'oeuvres are amazing. I can't stop eating. Maybe we should try and gather the team and make our way back. It's getting pretty late. I always feel responsible for Isabella. Although, she has more energy than any of us combined."

Cory chuckled. "Tell me about it. I wish I had that kind of energy, but yeah, I think we need to head back. We have an early meeting with the general tomorrow."

It took another hour to find Gale and drag her from the ball, but they finally made their way back to the carriage houses as they laughed and shared their stories of the evening. Marie chose not to share her experience with the mind reader. She wanted to meditate and confer with her spirit guides before coming to any conclusions. Dealing with vampires was something out of her depth, and she needed more guidance on the situation.

SERAFINO LOUNGED in his high wingback chair and contemplated the events of the evening. He knew the mistake that Nicolai made created a whole series of issues that brought this psychic into their house. There was no doubt he was dealing with a powerful medium, but that never bothered him because he loved a challenge.

He took a sip of blood and yelled across the room. "Clarice, bring me Nicolai."

Within a few minutes, a pale, frail Nicolai entered the room and bowed down in front of Serafino and whispered, "You called me my Lord?"

"Yes, I wanted to let you know that I will no longer need to teach you a lesson for taking my concubine and killing her."

Nicolai's spirits lifted as he grinned but continued to stare at the floor. "Thank you, my Lord. I grow weak, and I'm famished."

"Yes, I'll have Clarice bring you some food, but your punishment isn't quite over. I have some plans for you to rectify this latest debacle. It seems we have a mystic in our midst and I'm going to need you to do some spying for me. Do you think you can handle that?"

Nicolai bravely lifted his head. "Oh yes my Lord, I will do whatever you command me. I swear I'll make no more mistakes. You can trust me."

Serafino slammed his fist on the table as his voice vibrated the walls. "Silence, I'll hear no more of your insidious lies. If you botch this up for me, it'll be your head. Do you hear me Nicolai?"

Nicolai's body quivered in a fetal position as he whispered, "Yes, Master. I hear you."

"Good, now be off with you and find Clarice. Get your fill and regain your strength because you're going to need it."

Nicolai ran off as Serafino's hideous laugh echoed in his ears and throughout the mansion. The bellowing of his voice reminded everyone he was the master and that they were all expendable if they disobeyed him.

EIGHT

The team grudgingly awoke to eat and get ready for their early meeting with the general. Isabella continued chattering on about the clothing the general wore and how his British dialect sounded like it came from the eighteen hundreds.

"Isabella would you please stop going on about the general being from the nineteenth century. It's ridiculous, and so is this meeting we're having with him. I mean come on, since when did we get involved with vampires?" Gale took the last bite of her rye toast and washed it down with coffee.

"I'm just saying that it's pretty crazy that his name is exactly like the one in the story."

Jim asked, "So do you think he's a time traveler?"

Isabella excitedly jumped off the stool and walked over toward Jim. "Yes, that's what I was thinking." She saw everyone's stare, and then continued, "I'm serious. I think there's something about him. He spoke like an aristocrat. Plus, if any of you had bothered to read the story, he was on the hunt for Carmilla because she killed his niece."

Marie could see this conversation was putting a

hold on everyone being ready in time for the meeting. "Look, we're not discounting anything, Isabella, but this isn't the time to get into it. We need to go, or we're going to be late. I don't know if the general is from the eighteen hundreds, but I do get the feeling he likes promptness."

"Okay, but I'm not giving up on this. I'm going to watch the general closely. Maybe I can use psychometry."

Marie snapped her head around and looked right at Isabella. "Absolutely not, I've told you before that we cannot use people for personal gain in that fashion. It isn't ethical. They need to give us consent."

Isabella stopped smiling. "Okay, I won't do anything, but don't you think that's a little ironic?"

Marie replied, "What is?"

"That we can't do anything without someone's consent the same way as vampires."

Mimi's eyes got large as her eyebrows went up. "I think I've had enough of this conversation. You're all giving me the chills."

"Yeah really, I think it's time we head out." Gale grabbed her purse and strutted out the door.

Marie could see Isabella's deflated reaction and walked over and draped her arm around Isabella's shoulders. "We love your enthusiasm, and you know that we defend each other and never discount anyone's ideas or theories. Let's just take this one step at a time and see what we can learn from General Spielsdorf. I promise that if I pick up anything odd or peculiar, I'll be the first to apologize for any of us disregarding what you believe."

Isabella grinned wide and hugged Marie. "Thank

you. I know I go on and on, but there's just something about the general that has my curiosity piqued."

Marie chuckled as she led Isabella outside and then locked the door behind them. "Oh yes, I can relate to curiosity. What do you think has gotten me into so much trouble this far?"

The team got into their cars and made their way back to The Olde Pink House for their meeting. Marie got a chill on her neck as she tried to shrug off the feeling that someone was watching her as she got into the passenger side of the SUV.

Cory asked, "Are you okay? You look a bit...spooked."

"Yeah, I don't know. I get the feeling I'm being watched." Marie looked in all directions and then smiled at Cory. "Never mind; I'm just a bit jumpy. All of this talk of vampires is unnerving."

"Did you get any guidance from your spirit guides for what happened at the ball?"

Isabella lunged toward the front seat and stuck her head between Cory and Marie. "What happened at the ball?"

Marie gave Cory a '*we weren't supposed to say anything*' type of look, and then turned her attention to Isabella. "I hadn't planned on sharing this with the team yet, but after we met with the general and returned to the ball, I felt someone willing me to look at them. It was someone across the room. I could feel them trying to read my mind and then vanished."

"You mean vanished into thin air?"

"No, no I mean...I'm not sure what I mean. Whoever it was disappeared rather suddenly." Marie shrugged her shoulders at Cory and continued, "Let's just keep this between us. I'm still trying to sort this out, and I didn't get the chance to meditate on it yet, and I'm not getting anything to help me better understand any of this. It's a bit frustrating."

"I won't tell anyone, but you have to admit some bizarre things are going on. Just like the guy in your vision wouldn't let you see his face."

The SUV came to a stop as Marie realized they had arrived. She unfastened her seatbelt and turned around toward Isabella. "Remember, we need to keep this to ourselves for right now. I don't always reveal everything to the team. I like to have my ducks in a row, as they say."

Isabella jumped out of the SUV and slammed the door shut. "Gotcha, my lips are sealed."

Gale approached them and said, "Why are you keeping your lips sealed?"

"I promised not to talk any more about the general and time travel."

"Good, because that whole conversation was starting to get on my nerves." Gale flipped her hair over her shoulder and rolled her eyes.

Isabella grinned and muttered under her breath. "Everything gets on your nerves."

"What'd you say?" Gale picked up the pace and tried to catch up with Isabella as she strutted on her six-inch wedged sandals.

Marie watched them continue their argument as they made their way to the side door of the house. "I swear Gale is like having another child around."

Cory grinned. "It's always an adventure."

The team made their way back down to the basement and found the general sitting in the same chair against the fireplace furiously writing in a small leather-bound journal. Again he was unaware of their presence until Marie cleared her throat and he picked up his head to look over his oval wire-rimmed glasses.

"Good morning to you all. Please have a seat. I took the liberty of ordering some coffee and croissants." Baron set his quill pen in the crease of his journal as it closed on its own.

Marie replied, "Good morning to you, General Spielsdorf. We appreciate you meeting with us again."

"Please, call me Baron. No need for formalities. So what is it that you would like to learn about vampires?"

Marie pulled out her chair and sat right next to him and jumped right in with questions that had been plaguing her mind for the last few days. "First, I guess I need to ask if vampires are real."

The general leaned back in his chair as he removed his glasses and set them on the table next to the journal. "May I call you Marie?"

"Of course, please do."

"Marie, I feel I have studied a lifetime on this subject. I'm growing older and weary of the hunt. You see, without dancing around the subject, my niece was turned by a vampire." The general saw eight pairs of eyes staring a hole through his head as he continued, "Yes, I know that sounds incredibly absurd, but I tell you the truth. I witnessed her transformation and tried to kill her myself."

Harry, dressed in his usual wrinkled three-piece suit, dropped his spoon, which caused everyone to jump. "Pardon me; I didn't mean to startle everyone. Did you just say you tried to murder your niece?"

"Yes, I did. Of course, in those days, it was a bit easier to do than what it is now."

Isabella piped up and asked, "Are you a time traveler?"

Marie scolded her. "Isabella, we asked you to drop that subject, remember?"

Baron gracefully turned his attention to Isabella and softly smiled. "She was about your age, my niece. Her name was Bertha Rheinfeldt. She had a great laugh and was full of life and enthusiasm. She played the harpsichord beautifully. That's what you call the piano today."

Isabella's eyes grew large as she leaned forward. "That's the name of the young girl in the book called Carmilla."

The general patted Isabella's hand and nodded. "Yes, that is correct. The so-called story of fiction is true. When I discovered how she had died, I knew what I had to do. It was a horrible experience, one that put me into a deep depression. But I had vowed that I would never stop hunting Carmilla after what she had done to my niece, as well as so many countless other innocent people over the centuries."

Marie noticed that Isabella's hand was still under the general's when she began to sway almost causing her to fall onto the floor. Marie shot out of her chair and quickly grabbed Isabella's shoulders and leaned her against her chest. "Isabella, are you okay?"

The general quickly removed his hand and stood up to retrieve a pitcher of water and poured the iced liquid into a glass. "Here, she'll need some water."

Marie stared at the general and then took the glass from him as Isabella slowly began to open her eyes. "Here, drink some water. Are you okay? What happened?"

She took a sip of water and then stared at the general and lifted her head as she tried to compose herself to sit upright in the chair. "The second your hand touched mine I felt a surge of energy and sensed deep sadness. The next thing I saw was a quick snippet of images of horrible things."

Baron replied, "I'm sorry my dear. I had no idea you were a mystic. I wouldn't have touched you if I had known."

Gale walked closer to Isabella and abruptly interrupted the conversation as she glared at the general. "You never answered her question."

Baron replied, "What question is that?"

"Are you a time traveler?"

The general gave a sweet smile. "My dear, I would have thought that was obvious. Yes, of course, I'm a time traveler. And apparently, I was to meet all of you so we can finally take down Carmilla."

Tim stood up and leaned his hands on the table. "Whoa, just a minute, what the hell do you mean take down Carmilla? I think we all need to regroup and start from the beginning. I wasn't quite sure if I believed in vampires, but now add to the fact of time travel, this is getting a bit out of hand."

"I think we can all agree to that." Cory remained seated as he glanced around at the team and then placed his attention on the general. "Sir, I believe you need to explain yourself."

The general released a heavy sigh and sat back down in his chair. "Yes, I know this all sounds a bit incredulous."

Mimi said, "You've got that right."

The general placed his glasses back on his face and opened the journal. He rummaged to the beginning and began reading. "I'll try to be as brief as I can. Who among you have read the story?"

Isabella replied, "I have, and I've shared it with everyone here."

"Yes, but I'm afraid we all haven't paid much attention to Isabella and the story, and for that, we apologize to her." Marie gave Isabella a warm apologetic smile and then looked at the general. "Baron, can you try to summarize what exactly happened to your niece, and how it is you came to be in the twenty-first century?"

"I'll do my best."

The general began to explain to the team how he and his niece had a chance meeting of a countess who begged them to look after her daughter, Millarca, while she needed to travel further. The countess was desperate for their help and they agreed to take her into their care until the countess returned. Millarca had become very close to them and shared many confidences of her life. She brought such amusement into their sometimes-lonely evenings at home.

He went on to say that on one particular evening at a ball, which lasted until the sun came up, she had become lost. He thought she got lost in amongst the crowd or in the extensive grounds surrounding them. They went into a desperate search, to no avail. It wasn't until the next day around two in the afternoon that their maid had found the missing girl in her room in a deep sleep due to her exhaustion of the long night.

Isabella said, "You didn't tell them the reason why the countess left Millarca with you."

Baron replied, "Yes you're quite right. It was due to

languor, the weakness that remained after her late illness. Because of this illness, she never emerged from her bedroom until the late afternoon. We also discovered that she locked her room from the inside and never disturbed the key until she needed assistance from our maid. There were even times when she was seen walking in the early mornings in some trance. We could never understand how she escaped from the room without leaving through the door or the barred windows."

Jim asked, "Did you ever suspect her being a vampire?"

"Not at that moment, no, but it was during this time that my niece, Bertha, began to lose her looks and health and started to have haunting dreams by a specter resembling Millarca. Sometimes in the shape of a beast."

"What's a specter?" Gale looked around the room. "What, you all know what it means?"

"Forgive me. I find it hard to speak in your twenty-first century English. It means a ghost." Baron pushed his glasses up the bridge of his nose and turned the page in his journal and continued, "Bertha began to have peculiar sensations happen to her, such as an icy stream running across her breast. At a later time, she felt the impression of needles pierce her at the throat. After a few nights, she felt as if she was being strangled and losing consciousness. I had two physicians attend to her, and neither were able to give me any definitive answers to her illness at that time. However, the one physician left me a note and instructed me to open it with a clergyman. The priest was not available, so I opened it myself.

I thought the physician had gone mad. His written note explained that a vampire had visited my niece. He instructed me to wait in hiding in my niece's room, which I did that evening. To my horror, a dark figure appeared at the foot of her bed and then swiftly ascended over her body and began to suck at her throat. I couldn't move at first, but then I lunged out with my sword and struck at the beast. It sprang toward the door, and I struck again, causing no infliction whatsoever. In a brief moment, I was able to make out Millarca's distorted face. She and the beast were one and the same. The creature disappeared, and shortly after that, my niece passed in her sleep."

"Are you serious right now? I can't believe any of this." Gale stood up from the chair and poured another cup of coffee that was set out on a side table.

"I know it is hard to believe, but it is true." The general looked at Isabella. "Did you understand that Millarca was an anagram of Carmilla?"

Isabella nodded, "Yes, I did. But I don't understand, in the story, you beheaded Carmilla and drove a stake through her heart and burned her remains."

Baron closed his journal. "The story you read was fiction in that explanation. I was not able to behead her. We were only able to drive a stake into her heart, which only paralyzed her. One of her ghouls was able to pull it out, and she was able to escape our grasp. My ancestors before me were vampire hunters, so I too must carry on the tradition and avenge my niece."

Cory stood up and stretched his back and walked over to the fireplace and leaned his arm on the mantle. "So you're telling us that vampires do exist."

"That is correct."

Mimi said, "So how the hell did you bring yourself from the nineteenth century through time travel?"

"I, unfortunately, do not understand the complete science of time travel. I believe I read of Einstein's theory of traveling at the speed of light away from earth and wormholes in space." Baron saw the blank looks on everyone's faces and then continued, "For me, it was the reading of my ancestor's journals that had experienced a strange occurrence take place with the wormhole effect in one of our family plots. The journals specifically gave directions of a wormhole at one of the particular tombstones there and that it had to occur during a full moon and the summer solstice."

Isabella feeling more refreshed asked, "Will you ever be able to go back?"

"Yes, the journals explain that it needs to be at the same spot. I will need to journey back to my family plot during the summer solstice and full moon."

Harry took a drink of water and looked at his watch. "I'm afraid you've missed that timeframe."

"Yes, that is true, but my work is not complete. We simply must find and kill Millarca, or Carmilla as she is known, and behead her."

Marie's brow furrowed as she leaned back in her chair. "I'm afraid we're a long way from her burial plot."

Baron removed his glasses and set them on the table and began to rub his eyes. "Do not worry. She's able to travel in time as well. We simply need to find her resting place here in Savannah."

Tim looked at Gale and then set his attention on the general. "And you know where this is?"

"I believe I've narrowed it down to two cemeteries. Anyone in the mood for a vampire hunt?"

NINE

Jim began shaking his head and ran his hand through his remaining hair. "Look, I was sort of on the fence of believing in vampires, but I'm afraid I'm having a hard time believing in any of this."

"I think we all are." Cory walked over next to Marie and grabbed her hand.

"I have no doubt you don't believe me, but what I say is true," said Baron. "Would it be possible for me to listen to the recording you have from your investigation? After all, that's why we were meeting here this morning."

Marie leaned down and began to unzip her laptop case. "Yes, of course, I think it may be helpful. I do have another question. Have you heard about what took place in the Tanners' barn and the body of a woman they found on Tybee Island?"

"Yes, I read the news articles. I'm not quite sure I believe a vampire killed one of their pigs. They only feed on animals when it is necessary. It would have been because they were in desperate need of feeding." The general took the headphones that Marie handed to him and began to inspect them. "As far as the woman found on the beach, that could be more in the lines of vampirism, but the stories of just leaving two puncture wounds in the neck aren't what I have witnessed in the past. The destruction of a vampire feeding is quite hideous. I do hope whoever is around her this evening is careful."

Isabella asked, "Why is that?"

"Because by now she'll have begun to turn and whoever is in her presence is in danger."

Cory quickly set his coffee cup down and grabbed his hat. "I'd better get over there."

Marie grabbed Cory's arm. "And just how do you propose to explain that to anyone? They'll think you're nuts. I certainly don't want you around her if that happens."

Gale couldn't keep the frustration from showing on her face. "Are you two seriously buying into all of this? "

"I have no choice. As I've said, I need to have facts, but with all that we've been through together, there has to be some belief in the paranormal. I'm just going to go back and see if they've come up with anything new on the case. They told me to stay in touch. I can check if anything else is going on at the ME's office." Cory kissed Marie's cheek. "I promise to be careful, and I promise to stay in touch with you."

Marie said, "You'd better. We'll do the same on our end."

The general was fiddling around with the headphones trying to adjust them on his head. "Can you please let me hear the recording?"

Gale snapped one of the ear pads in place startling the general. "You could be a little more patient."

Marie glared at Gale. "Gale please don't be so

rude. I'm sorry Baron. Just let me plug this in and find the right recording."

After a few minutes, Baron removed the headphones and rubbed his eyes. "That's Carmilla. I recognize her voice. She's here in Savannah. I think we need to organize a hunt to find her as soon as possible. We can't waste any time."

Harry tried to straighten his tie as he stood up from his chair and walked over to the table and grabbed a croissant. "General Spielsdorf, I am a believer in many things because I've witnessed them myself over the years, but I'm afraid that I know nothing of hunting vampires. If what you say is true and from all the myths and folklore I've read about them, I believe we need to know what we're doing to hunt and kill a vampire. Wouldn't you agree?"

"Of course, I agree. I have had years of experience, as well as guidance from my ancestors. I can certainly instruct you all on the subject."

Gale sat back down next to Tim and began rolling up the headphone cord. "Let me ask you this, what exactly happened to your ancestors? I mean, how many of them survived hunting down vampires? I'm not sure I trust you as an authority on this subject."

The general smiled at Gale. "I like your tenacity. I believe you'll do just fine. As far as my ancestors, yes some of them lost their lives, while others were victorious in wiping out smaller covens. But nobody has been able to stay on the trail of Carmilla. This is the closest I've been. I understand if none of you wish to help me, but I simply cannot waste any more time because you're all likely to witness many more deaths and transitions take place in this beautiful historic town."

Marie gathered her laptop and placed it in its case. "If you don't mind, I think we all need to regroup and have a very much needed conversation. We only came here to help the Tanners and if you don't believe vampires had anything to do with that, well then, I'm not sure how much further we wish to continue in your quest. I hope you understand."

The general stood up and bowed his head. "Of course I understand. If you should decide to join me, I'll be at the Bonaventure Cemetery tonight before dusk. This will be the first place I'll search. If nothing develops there, I'll then go to the Colonial Park Cemetery."

Gale asked, "When exactly is dusk? I mean, just state a time."

The general replied, "It's just before the sun begins to set. Contrary to the myths of sunlight for vampires, most varieties can walk in sunlight. A few can't. Some can only do so if they've fed within the last twenty-four hours, others can at will. Most lose the majority of their abilities in direct sunlight, and all are at least mildly photosensitive, which is why it is best to hunt them in their resting place. It increases our chances to defeat them."

"I read that you need to be careful of any traps, or vampires who are on watch during their sleep." Isabella rummaged through her iPad to search for more information.

"That's very true, Isabella, that is why we need to have the right tools to defeat them when they are at their weakest."

Gale clicked her tongue and rolled her eyes. "I think you're a loon."

Marie grabbed Gale's arm and dragged her out of

the room. "Come on everyone. Let's get back to the carriage houses. I need to check on Bailey."

Isabella was the last to leave as she lingered in the doorway. "General Spielsdorf, what's it like to time travel?"

Baron politely smiled and said, "It's quite disorienting. You tend to feel as though your head is swimming in a fog."

"If we don't meet up with you tonight, I wish you luck in finding Carmilla, and I hope that you have a safe journey back to your time."

"Thank you my dear, and I wish you well also."

Isabella heard her name called by Marie and hurriedly ran up the stairs when she began to sweat and became dizzy as she tried to grab the railing. Before she could yell for Marie, her head began to ache, and everything went dark.

Carmilla knew she could control the young mystic's mind as she chuckled to herself. It was easier than she had thought once she realized the young fool's mind was open and easy to read. It was amusing to see that Baron was hot on her trail, but she knew him to be a fool and planned on ending his journey through time. She slowly released the young mystic's thoughts and decided to gain her strength back through sleep as she closed her eyes and drifted into a trance.

"Isabella, are you okay? Answer me." Marie shook her shoulders and tried to wake her.

Isabella slowly opened her eyes as she tried to

focus on Marie's mouth. "Where am I? What happened? I remember running up the stairs, and I got dizzy, and then everything went dark."

Mimi handed a bottle of water to Isabella. "Drink this and stay seated. You don't want to pass out again."

"Thank you, Mimi." Isabella gulped down the water and then screwed on the lid. "It was the craziest thing. When everything went dark, I felt like I was laying somewhere that was cold and damp. It smelled like mold or mildew, and dirt."

Tim helped Isabella stand but kept his arm around her waist. "Are you okay to walk back up the stairs?"

"I think so." Isabella looked at Marie with wide eyes. "Marie, I think someone was reading my mind, but I can't remember any of those thoughts. It was creepy."

Marie left out a sigh and lovingly rubbed Isabella's arm. "Don't worry about any of that right now. You gave us quite a scare. We need to get you back to the house so you can lie down."

Gale looked over at Baron standing in the doorway. "Where were you when she fell?"

Baron sheepishly looked at Isabella. "I'm sorry, but I wasn't aware she fell. I didn't hear anything until just now."

Gale replied, "Really, that sounds convenient."

"Gale, please, this isn't the time." Marie looked at the general. "I'm sorry, she tends to speak her mind."

"No, I take no offense. I believe in speaking your mind. I promise you that I was deep in thought with taking notes in my journal." The general looked back at Isabella. "Did you say it felt as though you could smell dirt and that someone was reading your mind?"

"Yes, it was peculiar and creepy."

"I'm afraid this doesn't sound good." The general walked from the doorway and entered the other room and then returned holding his journal. He flipped through to the middle and ran his finger down the page. "If this is what I think it is, then Carmilla is on to me. More than likely she was able to read Isabella's mind and pick up on the last conversation she had, which was with me."

Harry asked, "What was the topic of your conversation?"

"We were chatting about me looking for Carmilla and time travel." The general closed the leather bound book and slipped it into his jacket pocket. "As much as I hate to ask this, I believe I'm going to need reinforcements. Her coven will now be at the ready."

"You don't even know what cemetery she's in." Gale strutted past the general and stood next to Tim and Isabella.

"You are correct, but I have a theory." The general looked at Marie and Isabella. "You both have the ability as psychics to tap into the mind of Carmilla, or one of her ghouls. You could lead us to where she beds down during the day."

"Absolutely not! I will not expose Isabella to any of this." Marie guided Isabella back into the room and had her sit down.

Baron followed at Marie's heels. "It is already too late, Carmilla has entered her mind. They are now connected."

Harry loosened his bow tie and sat down next to Isabella. "I'm in agreement with Marie. If what you say is true and there has been a connection, then I'm not comfortable with allowing Isabella to interact with Carmilla."

"But I want to help, can't I do this if I want to?"

Marie shook her head. "I'm sorry Isabella. I promised your mother that I would protect you while you're in my care. I won't allow this. We need to leave now because you and I need to do a protection meditation. I need to make sure she can't do this to you again."

Baron patted Isabella's hand and then gently lifted her chin. "You must listen to Marie while you are in her care. I'm sorry to have mentioned it."

Isabella dropped her lower lip and tried to gain some sympathy. "Rats, I never get to have any fun."

Marie grabbed her laptop case and slung the strap over her shoulder. "Come on everyone. I'd like to get back and take Bailey for a walk and then check in with Cory. Baron, as far as having someone handle the mind reading, I'll be glad to help."

Gale glared at Marie. "Are you serious? First of all, I still don't think any of this is real, and if it is, I don't think you should be getting involved either. You have no idea what vampires are capable of while reading minds, and if this Carmilla is still banging around from the nineteenth century, then apparently she's got a lot of power on her side."

Mimi shook her head in agreement. "I'm going to have to agree with Gale. I don't think Cory's going to allow it either."

Baron took a sip of coffee and wiped his mouth with a cloth napkin. "I'll be staying here if anyone should decide to join me. I can reach out to a few locals who have helped me before, but the more, the better."

Gale shook her head and started toward the doorway and up the stairs as she shouted over her shoulder. "I still think you're a loon."

The team said their goodbyes and made sure they kept a close watch on Isabella going up the stairs. As they made their way to the cars, Marie got a shiver up her spine, and her senses became heightened. She looked in all directions before getting behind the wheel of the SUV. Her primary focus was to protect Isabella. She just couldn't allow anyone or anything to try and enter her mind again.

TEN

THE TEAM ARRIVED BACK at lunchtime and decided to order take-out pizza from Vinnie's place. Cory arrived shortly afterward and welcomed the smell of cheese, pepperoni, and marinara sauce.

Marie and the team filled Cory in on what took place with the general and how Isabella may have had her thoughts compromised. Cory began to explain what he learned at the ME's office and that they still had no clue exactly how the young woman died. There had been some bruising around her neck, so the ME speculated a possible strangling but hadn't been able to pinpoint the puncture wounds.

"When will they know the final results from their lab?" Marie kept a close watch on Isabella as she bit into a piece of cheese pizza and closed her eyes at the explosion of flavors taking place in her mouth.

"They put a rush on the results, so they hope to have them later today. Tiffany promised to give me a call when she got the final report." Cory chugged down some iced tea and leaned in toward Marie and Isabella. "Are you two sure you're okay? I know how draining this is on your minds, as well as taxing on your bodies. Apparently, whoever this is, has tried tapping into both of your thoughts."

Gale shot forward on the couch and looked at Cory. "What do you mean both of their thoughts?" She then turned her attention toward Marie. "Did this happen to you too?"

Marie gave that look to Cory and then put the pizza down on her paper towel. "Yes, this happened to me at the ball. After our meeting with the general as I made my way back to the ball, I sensed someone across the room trying to enter my mind. I willed them to turn around, but they disappeared."

"Vanished into thin air." Isabella caught Marie's glare and said, "Sorry."

Tim gave his crust to Bailey and grabbed another piece of pepperoni pizza. "What do you mean vanished? And why didn't you share any of this with the rest of us?"

"Because I was trying to get a handle on it before I told any of you. Isabella happened to hear our conversation in the car earlier. I wanted to meditate on it more to try and find out exactly what my spirit guides could tell me. But with all that has happened this morning, I haven't had a moment to quiet my mind. After we finish eating, and Isabella has had a chance to rest, we're both going to meditate and protect ourselves."

"I think that's a good and important thing to do." Harry tried to wipe a blob of sauce from his shirt with his finger but only made the stain worse. He gave up on the idea and continued, "Without adding any more fuel to the fire, what are we going to do about General Spielsdorf and his need for our help?"

Cory replied, "I think it's a terrible idea. The general stated that he didn't feel a vampire slaughtered the pig, and he wasn't completely sure the young woman was either. I'm not sure how I feel about time travel and this whole theory of hunting down a character from a nineteenth-century fiction book."

"I'm with you, Cory. I think this guy is a nut job looking for attention. He's lonely and obviously lacks the skillset to get along with people." Gale snagged a piece of pepperoni from Tim's pizza and popped it in her mouth.

"I believe him, whether any of you do or don't. It's just a feeling I have." Isabella shimmied herself down into the love seat and laid her head on the overstuffed arm.

Mimi munched on a peach as she quickly wiped the juice from her chin with the back of her hand. "Maybe somebody needs to go back to the morgue to watch and see if the young woman becomes a vampire."

"Are we seriously thinking this right now? Come on people, this is ridiculous. Look, we came here to do an investigation for the Tanners, and we were able to help them feel a little more relieved that their daughter isn't nuts. We didn't come here for anything else. There's no proof of vampires killing pigs or women, so why are we venturing into this ridiculous idea of vampires?" Gale's leg shifted when Bailey nudged his rump against her calf as she smiled and began to stroke his neck.

Jim replied, "We get the idea that you don't believe in any of this, but I'm inclined to give the general some slack. I think we need to regroup after Marie and Isabella do some meditation before we rule any of this out, just my two-cents on the subject."

Tim said, "Maybe the general is a vampire."

Isabella frowned at the group and moved into a seated position. "If some of you think this is a waste of time, then maybe we should go home. I'm not going to try and convince anyone that what happened to me back there was real. I know what I felt. I know someone tried to take over my mind. Why is it when Marie has an experience like this, you all jump on the bandwagon and support her? Where's the support for me?"

Marie's heart sank as she quickly gave a side-glance at Cory and then moved closer to Isabella and draped her arm around her shoulders. "You're right. We are going to support yours and Baron's theory, and we do believe that someone tried to read your mind. Whether it was Carmilla or not, I think we need to follow through with finalizing this case."

Jim asked, "What's our next move?"

"Isabella and I are going to meditate and do a protection prayer. I think all of us need to do one, just as we always do before an investigation." Marie stood up and walked over to Cory. "Cory, I think you need to go back to the morgue and wait for the results, and if need be, wait to see if anything does happen to that woman."

"What will the rest of us do?" Tim downed the last piece of pepperoni pizza and wiped his mouth with a paper napkin.

"Why we're going to hunt for vampires, of course." Marie smiled at Isabella's beaming face. "Those of you that wish to go, that is. I have no idea if what the general has told us is true, but he did ask for our help, and we are in the business of helping others, right? So I say we meet him before dusk, which according to my weather app, would be around seven tonight. That should give us roughly two hours before the sun sets."

"And do you think two hours is enough to hunt for vampires?" Gale said flippantly.

"I don't know, Gale, but you're more than welcome to stay here while we find out." Marie stood up and gently took Isabella by the elbow. "Come on. We can use the back room of the other carriage house to meditate. I suggest the rest of you start to research what we need as weapons to go on this hunt."

Cory's eyebrows went up. "I guess I'll head back over to the morgue, but I'll be meeting you at the cemetery. I'm not waiting around to see if this woman turns. I need to be there just in case General Spielsdorf's claims are true."

Isabella stood a little taller and then made a *told you so* face at Gale. "Looks like we're going vampire hunting."

Gale shrugged her shoulders and gave Isabella a nonchalant look. "Whatever, I'll come along so I can say, told you so, when nothing turns up tonight."

"You're just afraid to stay here alone." Mimi chuckled as she threw her peach seed into the garbage. "Marie, would you like me to ask if Margaret wants to come along? She might be a helpful addition."

"Sure, why not? The more we have, the merrier." Marie smiled as she followed Isabella toward the door and kissed Cory on the cheek along the way. "See you all in a little while."

. . .

Marie and Isabella were able to meditate and ask their spirit guides for protection during the vampire hunt. Again, Marie's spirit guides told her there were real and disguised vampires who were equally dangerous. Gracie warned Isabella that the undead was in complete chaos and they were aware of a war going to take place.

While some of the team haphazardly searched for information on how to destroy a vampire, they determined it would be quite difficult to find wooden stakes and silver swords in the local stores.

Harry visited the Cathedral of St. John the Baptist and obtained, with the help of a priest, several vials of holy water. He wouldn't convey how he enacted this endeavor, but nobody seemed to mind having the small bottle of the liquid.

Tim visited a Christian store and purchased ten crosses for everyone and then took them to another priest at a Catholic church down the street from the carriage houses to be blessed.

It was half-past six when they made their way to the Bonaventure Cemetery as each of them carried a vial of holy water and a blessed cross. Shortly after that, Cory arrived and accepted the tools for his protection.

Tim walked toward the tall wrought iron gate and instinctively grabbed Gale's hand. "I do wish we had some stakes and swords. I feel like we're going into a gunfight with a water pistol. I think we're going to have to climb over the fence since the cemetery closed at five."

After clumsily climbing the fence, they cautiously made their way along the main road. The Spanish moss covered the live oak trees, which eerily took on the look of creepy Halloween decorations. Before they continued any further, they saw General Spielsdorf standing next to an imposing macabre mausoleum. He reached down into a large canvas sack and pulled out several wooden stakes and laid them on the ground. From the corner of his eye, he caught the group huddled in a bunch as he smiled and nodded his head.

"So good of you to come. I'm pleased to have the extra hands this evening. I have more stakes in that sack and a few silver swords stacked against the wall of the mausoleum. Didn't Margaret come with you?"

Mimi replied, "No, she had another engagement this evening."

Cory asked, "Where did you get all of these and how did you know how many to bring?"

Isabella dropped her head and began to scuff her foot against the wall of the mausoleum. "Sorry, I gave him a call and told him we were coming."

The corner of Marie's mouth went up as she grabbed the tip of Isabella's chin and lifted her face. "That was a brilliant thing to do. Now we're equipped."

Isabella smiled and swiftly grabbed one of the stakes and began to roll it in her hands. "That's why I called him. I knew we needed to prepare for this. I'm glad you're not mad."

"I'm not sure why we didn't call him ourselves." Mimi winked at Isabella and then made her way over to the swords and tried to lift it with one hand. "Wow, these things are heavy."

"Yes, they're made of pure silver. I believe we'll save those for the menfolk to carry because I only have four. It can stop them temporarily when used to cut or wound their extremities, but they're fatal when it penetrates their heart or when you chop off their head."

"I won't be using a sword." Gale grabbed a stake and propped it on her shoulder as if holding a rifle at shoulder arms.

Harry grabbed a sword and carefully set the tip on the ground and began to inspect the intricate detail of the handle. "With only four swords, Baron, what are you using?"

The general carefully pulled out a silver-plated handgun and set it in the palm of his hand. "I had a friend of mine from this century, let's call him a military man, who modified this Beretta 92FS Inox pistol. You can see how he converted it to full auto with extended magazines and large compensators that extend all the way back along the frame to the trigger guard. It can shoot twenty-five to thirty rounds. It's all new to me, but he assured me this would do the job."

Cory asked, "May I?"

"Of course, the safety is on." The general allowed Cory to remove it from his palm.

Cory carefully examined the weapon and then handed it back to Baron. "What type of ammunition do you use?"

"Silver bullets, of course."

"Of course, what else would you use?" Gale shook her head and bent down to tighten the boot strings of her Indigo Road boot and tried to conceal a smile.

Marie ignored Gale's typical rudeness and directed her attention to the general. "Baron, I think you may need to give us a crash course in vampire hunting."

"I'll do the best I can in the short amount of time

that we have. We are losing daylight." The general handed out the rest of the stakes and flashlights and then proceeded to pick the lock on the wrought iron door of the mausoleum. "My hunch is that Carmilla is staying here and that she and her ghouls are aware that we are coming for her, so please be alert."

Jim's knuckles went white as he gripped the wooden stake in his right hand. "You're breaking into this mausoleum on a hunch?"

The general heard the click, turned the doorknob, and opened the heavy door. "My hunches are usually right."

Gale turned on her flashlight and leaned against Tim's bulging biceps as they entered the dark, damp mausoleum single file. "I like how we're staking our lives on his hunches *usually* being right."

Marie said, "Gale would you please shush so we can listen to Baron?"

Cory turned toward Isabella and put his hands on her shoulders. "Isabella, the team and I want you to stay here. I know this isn't what you want, and you're about to give me a line of how you can help psychically, but we simply will not put you in any danger. We have no idea what we're walking into, and we'd never forgive ourselves."

Isabella tried to keep the tears from falling down her cheeks as she shrugged away from Cory and turned toward Marie. "Do you agree?"

"Yes, I do, and we need you here to alert anyone if something happens. You are still playing an important role, Isabella." Marie wiped the tears from Isabella's cheeks and then pulled her to her chest. "I simply couldn't bear it if anything happened to you. Please know we're doing this for your safety."

Isabella looked up at Marie's face, and then looked around at the group all staring back with concerned looks on their faces. "Alright, what do you need me to do?"

Marie squeezed Isabella and smiled. "Thank you for being so grown up. Please pay attention to anything odd that may happen and call this number if needed. It's Tiffany's direct line. Mimi is going to stay with you."

"Okay, but I'm keeping the cross, stake, and holy water just in case. Maybe I can try to see the gravesite of Gracie."

"First of all, no you won't go traipsing about looking for Gracie's gravesite. We can do that together. And yes, both of you will need to keep some tools to defend yourselves." Marie turned and winked at Cory and then picked up a stake and shifted the cross in her pocket. "Okay everyone, let's go."

Baron stooped and began to search through his sack and pulled out three long wooden sticks with burlap cloth wrapped around the ends, which smelled of kerosene. He handed one to Tim and Cory and kept one for himself and then proceeded to light them. The flames created a popping sound and shot out from the tips as it illuminated a staircase on the other side of the mausoleum.

Gale tried to keep her lip from trembling, as she looked wide-eyed at Tim. "You mean to tell me we're going down those stairs? Since when do mausoleums have stairs in them?"

Baron turned toward the group and held his torch out to the side. "Yes, we need to go down these stairs. They should lead to an underground tomb where I believe Carmilla is hiding."

Harry said, "Don't you think we would have encountered her army of ghouls by now? I mean they'd be the ones out front protecting her."

"She's not in this particular tomb. We need to follow the underground tunnel to where she is hiding. I was able to retrieve a map of this section of the cemetery that shows where these tunnels connect family plots. I wanted to come in from the other side to hopefully create a surprise attack."

Gale clumsily shifted the stake into her left hand and tried to wipe the hair that was sticking to her forehead. "To this point, you haven't given me a whole lot of confidence with your hunches and hoping to create surprise attacks."

Baron began to walk toward the stairs with the group in tow as their bodies cast distorted shadows along the wall. "The first rule of vampire hunting is always to be alert and ready for anything. You must shine your lights all around you, especially above you. You never know where they are lurking.

Vampires have many different types of skillsets. They have excellent strength, speed, endurance and agility, superior senses, and high-level resistance to damage. Some have the psychic ability, such as you, Marie, being able to put their victims into a trance and read your mind. It's important to shut off your thoughts, especially fear."

Baron continued to lead them down the narrow passages, all the while swinging his torch up and in front of him as he kept a steady hand on his gun. "Some can transform into mist or even animals. Some are daytime walkers, which allows them to be out in the sunlight without being burned. These are the most dangerous because they are half human and half vampire, also known as a dhampir. They can be among us and we'd never know it. Although some dhampir's are vampire hunters themselves."

Gale stood close behind Marie and Cory as she tightened the grip on the cross in her hand. "Marie, didn't your spirit guides say that there were real and disguised vampires?"

"Yes, I'm not quite sure what that meant, but it is possible they were referring to a dhampir. Baron, what exactly do we need to do if we're confronted? I'm not sure any of us would be quick or strong enough to fight vampires."

"The first thing you need to do is show them your cross and stab them anywhere you can with the stake. You can throw the holy water in their eyes to temporarily blind them until one of us can take care of them."

Jim's scalp glistened against the torchlight as he moved closer to Marie as a line of defense. "I'm beginning to think this was a bad idea. I think we're out of our depth, just like the Clampetts trying to survive in Beverly Hills."

Baron reached the end of the tunnel first as he pointed toward another set of stairs. He placed his finger to his lips and whispered. "Let's remain vigilant."

Gale's body shivered in fear as she tightened her grip on the stake. "I think I just peed a little."

Baron led them slowly up the stairs as his torch illuminated the tomb. He pointed his gun to the left, signaling for Cory and Tim to make their way to the other side of a concrete-encased coffin.

Baron carefully peered over the edge and held his torch over the center. "It's empty."

ELEVEN

GALE SAID, "What, what do you mean it's empty? You can see in it?"

Marie stood next to Baron and peered into the sarcophagus. "He's right, nobody is in here, but it does look like somebody had been in it. There's fresh dirt lining the bottom."

"I believe it is probably Carmilla's native soil. They can only survive resting in their native soil." The general began to move his torch around the room to be sure there were no vampires in hiding.

"Okay, that's creepy and a little hard to believe. Who would have brought the native soil, and where did it come from?" Gale moved closer to Tim but kept her back to the coffin to be sure she was ready to defend herself.

Harry began to run the soil through his fingers and then placed a palm full into a plastic bag he retrieved from his jacket pocket. "I had always thought the native soul was a myth. Either way, I think it would be wise to take a sample of this and test it."

Cory said, "What do we do now?"

The general turned toward the stairs and began to

leave the tomb. "We need to head over to the other cemetery. We're losing daylight."

Marie looked at Cory and then began to follow the general down the stairs. "If it's all the same to you, Baron, I think we'll call it a night. Cory needs to head back to the morgue to get the results from the autopsy, and we need to..."

Marie stopped short at the deafening shrill that echoed throughout the tomb. The cackle rose up from behind them, but there wasn't anyone in sight. They tried to cover their ears when the laughter stopped as quickly as it started, and the tomb became silent.

"What the hell was that?" Tim swung his stake and torch around in one swift movement.

"I believe Carmilla has outwitted us." Baron continued down the stairs with his head hung low.

Gale scurried after the general and made sure she was between him and Tim. "You don't mean to tell us that was Carmilla we just heard."

"Yes, that's who it was. She knew we were coming. There's no point going to the other cemetery. She won't be there. She's already moved her place of rest."

Harry sauntered up next to the general and tried to keep up with his steps. "Where do you think she may have gone?"

The general let out a heavy sigh as he continued to lead the group back down the dank halls and up the next set of stairs to the tomb where they began. "I have no idea. I can only hope she or her army makes a mistake."

Marie said, "What kind of a mistake would that be?"

"I'm not sure, to be honest." The general stopped in mid-step and looked directly into Marie's eyes. "I want to warn you though. You must keep an eye on Isabella. Carmilla has entered her mind, and she will not let up until she has taken it over."

"You don't think Isabella caused Carmilla's escape, do you?"

"I'm not sure, but I know how she operates, and she's capable of seducing. You must help Isabella to keep her mind closed, especially when she sleeps."

The group remained quiet as they made their way out of the tomb and watched in silence as the general locked the iron door. They tried to stay calm after hearing the sinister laugh presuming to have been made by Carmilla. The men placed their torches in the bucket of water the general had provided and then gave their stakes back to him as he slid them into his canvas bag and cinched it closed.

Isabella almost tripped over a tombstone as she hastily ran toward the group. "What happened? Did you find Carmilla? Were there any vampires down there? If not, are we going to another cemetery to hunt them?"

"Whoa, slow your roll. Remember when I said I was going to give you all the *I told you so* face...well, here it is. I told you so." Gale jammed the vial of holy water into her Levi's skinny jeans.

"You mean there weren't any vampires? No Carmilla?" Isabella slumped down onto an obelisk marble headstone and dropped her head into her hands. "Isn't any of this true?"

Marie gave her usual glare at Gale and walked over next to Isabella and sat down. "Isabella, you'll be glad and surprised to learn that although we didn't see Carmilla and her goons, we did have an interesting out of body visit."

"What do you mean?" Isabella slid to the edge of the monument and excitedly stared into Marie's eyes. "What happened?"

Harry began to roll down his shirt and suit coat sleeves as he walked over to where Marie and Isabella were sitting and pulled out the bag of soil. "The sarcophagus was empty except for this supposed native soil. We're going to have it tested."

Gale abruptly pushed past Harry. "Yeah, never mind the damn dirt. When we were heading out of the tomb, we heard the creepiest laugh that sent chills down my spine. Baron here seems to think it was Carmilla."

"Do you dispute my hypothesis?" The general carefully wrapped a chamois cloth around his pistol and then placed it into a nylon gun case and zipped it closed.

Marie replied, "We're not sure what to think, but we all heard that laugh."

"It was Carmilla." Cory slipped his cross back into his pants pocket and sheepishly looked up at everyone stares.

"My good man, why do you say that?" Baron's expression showed both surprise and relief.

"Because that's the voice I heard on our investigation. There's no mistaking it. It's the same voice we picked up on our recordings."

"Yes, it is." Tim nodded at Cory and then adjusted his baseball hat forward on his head.

Marie smiled at her husband and then looked back at the team. "I think we need to head back and document everything that happened this evening. Isabella, I need to help you learn how to close off your mind, even while you sleep. Baron has suggested that

Carmilla has a connection with you and has clever ways of entering your mind. We need to protect you from that."

Isabella swiftly stood up and again looked directly at Gale. "Who's saying I told you so now?"

"Yeah, yeah, yeah." Gale flipped her hair behind her shoulder and strutted back toward the vehicles.

Tim said, "I guess that means we're ready to go."

Cory chuckled. "I'd say so. I'm going back to the morgue. I'm curious about this autopsy report." He walked over to Marie and then kissed her cheek. "I'll see you back at the house. Be careful, please."

"I will. Okay, everyone. Let's go. Baron, you're welcome to join us. We could bone up for more information on how to hunt down vampires. There may be some leftover pizza."

"Thank you, but I'm going to have to decline. I need to enter everything into my journal and research some more things myself. I'll talk with you tomorrow. If I find anything, I'll be sure to let you know."

Marie replied, "And we'll do the same."

They said their goodbyes and made their way back to join Gale at the cars. Marie kept Isabella close to her side as she looked around in all directions trying to ward off that same feeling of being watched. No way in hell would she allow any harm to come to Isabella or anyone for that matter. That was a promise she planned to keep. All of this had a similar ring to it when Myra had been possessed and taken over by a demon. She simply refused to allow it to happen again.

. . .

IT WAS HALF-PAST seven when Marie awoke as she spotted Bailey's head resting on the bed. "Good morning boy," she whispered. "It's a good thing you weren't with us last night. I have enough trouble keeping the team out of harm's way."

"And I have trouble keeping you out of harm's way." Cory shifted on the bed and pulled himself up against the headboard.

Marie did the same and leaned forward and kissed him hard on the lips. "Good morning husband. That was quite the night, wasn't it?"

Cory rubbed the sleep from his eyes and returned the kiss. "Yes, I'd say it was another eventful night. Of course, all of these nights tend to run together. I'm not sure which one stands out more than the others."

"I know, and I was relentless last evening with Isabella making sure she was able to keep her mind clear. She's got quite the talent. I wish I had had someone to mentor me when I was her age. She's so much more open and eager to learn. That also may be the reason why Carmilla can enter her mind so easily." Marie continued rubbing Bailey's head. "You got back pretty late, and we didn't get to finish our conversation about the autopsy findings."

"There isn't much to report. The coroner didn't have any new answers to the bite marks in her neck, other than an animal bite or someone hooking her up to a machine and draining her blood, which I think is ridiculous. They're baffled on the cells of the remaining blood found on her neck. I'm not getting any detailed information, but I sensed from Tiffany that they're concerned and confused."

"I guess the body was still there?"

"As far as I know, but I thought Harry said it

would be a total of forty-eight hours until the full transformation into a vampire occurred." Cory swung his legs around from the bed and stood up to stretch.

"Look at you knowing all there is about vampirism." Marie chuckled and also got out of bed and walked over to Cory and wrapped her arms around his bare waist. "It turns me on."

Cory gently took Marie's face into his hands and lifted her lips to his. "You know Bailey is a mood killer. If we send him out of our room, he'll wake the others up wanting to go outside."

"Yeah, you're right, but I'll be glad when we're back home. It's been too many days if you know what I mean." Marie allowed Cory to trail gentle kisses down her neck as her knees grew weak and she leaned into his firm body.

"If we don't stop this right now, it isn't going to matter who's in the room with us."

They were interrupted by Bailey's bark and a knock on the door. Marie jumped and quickly slipped on her robe while Cory hastily found his shirt and pulled it over his head.

Marie opened the bedroom door to Isabella. "Good morning, is everything all right?"

"I'm not sure. I had the strangest dream last night. I did as you said and kept my mind blocked, but I think I picked up on where Carmilla may be going."

Marie's eyes grew wide as she tried to remain calm and casually looked at Cory and then put her arm around Isabella to guide her into the living room. "Okay, why don't we have some breakfast, and you can fill me in on what happened."

Cory replied, "I'll start the coffee and take Bailey out."

Marie chuckled at Bailey's wagging tail as he ran out of their room and straight to the outside door. "I think Bailey has the right idea. Isabella, I'll meet you in the kitchen in a minute."

Isabella smiled and made her way into the tiny kitchen. "I'll make some toast."

After everyone's bladders had been relieved, Marie, Cory, and Isabella sat on the stools surrounding the granite countered island and chatted about Isabella's dream.

"So you're telling me you felt as if you were just following along with Carmilla?" Marie sipped the hot java and then took a bite of toast slathered with raspberry jam.

Isabella replied, "It was more like it was me seeing it through Carmilla's eyes. I saw her point of view, and I have to say, it was creepy. But I was able to make out where she is hiding."

Cory filled Bailey's water bowl and set it on the floor next to his food dish. "Don't keep us in suspense. What did you see?"

"It's a bit odd, but the name on the sign was called The Pirates House." Isabella looked from Cory to Marie and waited for a response, and then continued, "I woke up wondering why it wasn't at a cemetery. But what I saw was a building sided with wood and brick. The sign read The Pirates House. So I looked it up, and it's a restaurant on Broad Street. It's supposedly haunted, and apparently, tunnels run underneath it to River Street. The picture on their website matches up with my dream."

Marie felt a shiver run down her spine as she tried to ward off the feeling of being watched. She took the last bite of her toast and washed it down with the remaining coffee. "Your theory is they went down into the tunnels?"

"I'm not sure because after I saw them enter the building, everything went dark."

"Do you think she suspected you were there?"

"I don't know. As soon as that stopped, I blocked my thoughts and fell back to sleep." Isabella felt Bailey's head against her leg as she smiled and gave him her last piece of toast.

Marie stood up and grabbed her plate and cup and placed them in the dishwasher. "Why don't we wake up the team and make our way back over to see Baron and fill him in on what you experienced? This new information could shed some light on his research. In the meantime, you make sure to clear your thoughts periodically as I showed you so as not to allow Carmilla to learn we may be on her trail."

Cory said, "Are we going to continue this hunt?"

"I don't know. What I'd like to do is have another chat with Mrs. Axelby and see if we can't find these so-called vampire clubs and talk to someone who claims to be a vampire. I'm still trying to piece together what my spirit guides mean by there being real and fake vampires and how they're both equally dangerous."

"While you're doing that, I'm going to head back to the station and see if Tiffany has any new information. They have been working around the clock." Cory got up from the stool and stood next to Isabella. "You be sure you listen to Marie. We don't need any more minds being taken over, you understand?"

Isabella smiled and nodded her head. "Yeah, I will, I promise."

"Good, now I'm going to take a shower. Tim

texted me a little while ago and said he and Gale would be up in a few minutes. I think they smelled the coffee."

"Why don't we make some more coffee for everyone and then get ready ourselves? I'll call Baron and give him a little insight into what happened and figure out when we can meet him." Marie bent down and grabbed Bailey's face in her hands and allowed him to lick her cheek. "You, my friend, are coming along today. I'm not going to keep you cooped up in here again."

The team assembled and went over the information about Isabella's dream, and they agreed there was more work to be done. They had to try and understand what happened to the Tanners' pig and to see if they could draw a connection to Carmilla.

Everyone was showered and ready to head over to talk with Baron for a ten o'clock meeting, while Marie continued to remain alert knowing for sure that someone was watching them.

SERAFINO HANDED the dead rabbit to Nicolai and smirked at the fledglings greedy devouring of the animal. "Nicolai you simply must learn to eat slower. You'll ruin your digestion."

Nicolai winced at Serafino's hideous laugh and only nodded as he continued to drain the animal of its blood. Once he had finished, he dropped the animal next to his knees and remained kneeling in front of his master. "I have much to report."

"Carry on then, tell me what you have learned."

Nicolai slowly raised his head and stared into his master's beady blood-red eyes. "The psychics and their followers have been meeting with the man Carmilla knows. They met at the Bonaventure Cemetery and went into the crypt. They didn't find her, of course, but they continue to meet to discuss plans for destroying the coven."

Serafino smiled and stared at the boy. "How did Carmilla escape them?"

"I believe she can read the young psychic's mind, but I also believe this psychic is tapping into Carmilla's thoughts." Nicolai slowly stood up and moved closer to Serafino. "Doesn't this make it difficult to remain secret, Master?"

Serafino pulled the boy closer to him and grabbed his chin so he could see his reflection in his eyes. "Yes, it does, and because of you, they are on our heels. Now go and learn things. I need to bring this situation to a close."

TWELVE

The team again found themselves sitting in the basement of the Olde Pink House discussing vampires and motives with the general. They were able to share Isabella's dream, and it matched with what the general had deciphered from his notes as to where they would be able to find Carmilla's new hiding place.

Marie was about to ask how they would organize another hunt when Cory and Harry almost collided with each other entering the room. "Hi, guys, you both seem to be in a hurry."

Harry looked at Cory and waved his hand toward the group. "Cory, please go first."

"No, you look like you were in a panic, by all means, you can go first."

Gale rolled her eyes and shook her head. "Oh for God's sake, someone go first."

Cory replied, "Very well, I will. I was able to get the lab results from our victim's blood. It seems as though the bloodstream consisted of a virus that came from a flea commonly found on cave-dwelling bats."

Tim almost dropped his cup of coffee as he struggled to keep it from spilling. "Did you just say bats?"

"Yes, I did, and that isn't all. The ME believes the victim was actually in a coma or a coma-like state."

Isabella asked, "You mean she isn't dead?"

Cory helped himself to a cup of coffee and sat on a stool next to Marie. "She is now, but from what they discovered, she was in a coma before she died. Nobody was able to detect it. This case has them completely baffled."

"That would be stage two of the vampirism process." The general looked around the room while trying to steady a biscuit between his fingers. "Within six to twelve hours of exposure, the victim develops a headache, fever, chills, and other flu-like symptoms, as well as a drastic increase in metabolism and cardiac output as the virus spreads throughout the body. These symptoms can be easily confused with more common infections, although the presence of bite wounds is usually enough to confirm the diagnosis. This stage lasts another six to twelve hours."

"But her body was found dead on Tybee Island." Mimi's apparent disgust of the topic of conversation made her refrain from finishing her coffee.

Baron said, "Nobody would have been around to notice if she was having these symptoms."

"Baron, what exactly happens in the second stage?" Marie rested her arm on Cory's thigh and gently squeezed his leg.

The general removed his wire-rimmed glasses from his nose and set them on top of his journal. "Within twenty-four hours of exposure, the victim will slip into a vampiric coma. Roughly ten hours into this phase, the pulse slows, breathing is shallow, and the pupils dilate. Many have been buried alive because of this. While the belief is that anyone infected with the virus turns into a vampire, only a small percentage of people survive vampiric comas. The young, old, and feeble never come out of their comas and eventually die, while the vast majority of survivors are males between the ages of eighteen to thirty-five. For that particular group, vampiric comas last about a day and typically end at night, but the former demographic may linger for an additional day or so before death."

Jim ran his hand over his balding head and then leaned back into his chair. "I'm guessing the third stage is turning into a vampire. Since our victim is female, will she survive and still transition?"

"Yes, the third stage is transformation, and she is in the right age limit. As far as her definitively turning, I suspect we'll have to wait."

Harry came out from behind the doorway after there had been a lull in the conversation and awkwardly shifted his sleeves up to his elbows. "With the timing you just stated, it looks as though our victim could turn at sunset tonight."

Marie said, "Harry, we're sorry. You had some news for us as well."

"Yes, I just came back from a local engineering firm where I have a friend who is one of their chief engineers. He specializes in environmental engineering and can test soil samples in their lab."

Gale looked at Harry, lifted her palms, and shrugged. "Well, don't leave us in suspense."

"From the ranges of the ph balance and toxicity, it appears the soil is from Austria."

Baron's eyes grew wide as he began to fumble

through his journal and tried to place his glasses back on his face. "If that is the case, Carmilla will not be able to keep hiding before she runs out of her native soil. They will have to travel back to Austria to retrieve more."

Isabella shifted her chair so she could directly face the general. "Who would be doing the retrieving?"

"Her loyal ghouls, of course." The general lowered his glasses to the tip of his nose and glanced over the rims at the group. "Time is of the essence. If Isabella's dream proves to be a vision and Carmilla has indeed fled to the tunnels under the restaurant, we must make our way to hunt her down before sunset tonight."

Cory's phone vibrated as he quickly retrieved it from his shirt pocket and took the call. "Hello Tiffany, how are you? Another victim? I see, yes, we can meet you there. I'll see you in ten."

Marie asked, "What was that about?"

"Another body was found along River Street, a forty-year-old male." Cory looked at Marie. "She asked if you and I could meet her there in ten minutes."

"Of course, let's go." Marie finished the last of her coffee and turned toward the group. "Why don't you all continue discussing whether we should accompany Baron this evening. Isabella, please be aware and keep your mind closed so we don't lose Carmilla's trail. We'll be back as soon as we can. Gale, please send me a text to let me know where you'll be when you leave here."

Gale replied, "Will do, and, Marie, be careful. I'm beginning to waiver on my thoughts that vampires aren't real. Plus, the tunnel under that restaurant empties out onto River Street. I think we can agree these two situations are not a coincidence."

"Yeah, I thought that too. Keep an eye on Isabella. She needs to be reminded every so often of her thoughts." Marie smiled at Gale and then followed Cory toward the stairs.

Cory reached the SUV first and opened Marie's door. "I do not like this case. I feel like my defenses are down."

Marie slid into her seat, shut the door, and proceeded to latch her seatbelt. "I know what you mean. I haven't said this to anyone, but I have the feeling of someone watching us."

"Since when?"

"Just the last couple of days. It makes me nervous not keeping an eye on Isabella." Marie turned toward Cory and tried to keep her emotions in check. "Cory, I simply cannot have anything happen to Isabella. I couldn't forgive myself. It brings up all the emotions when we lost Myra. I can't go through that again."

Cory came to a stop at a red light and grabbed Marie's hand. "We're not going to let anything happen to anyone. I promise you. We need to stay alert, and we need to find out a little more about these vampire groups. Have you had the chance to talk with Margaret?"

"Not yet, it's been a little nutty here lately." Marie chuckled and then turned her attention to the flashing lights ahead of them. "It looks like this is the spot. I'm getting tired of finding more bodies."

"You and me both."

The Savannah River waterfront along River Street contained century old buildings, cotton warehouses converted into antique shops, and spectacular pubs and restaurants. Anyone could take a paddle-wheel riverboat cruise, as well as watch the ships from around the world sail into one of the busiest ports in America.

Marie got out of the SUV and walked alongside Cory as she tried to assess the situation in front of her. There appeared to be two separate areas covered with a sheet, one longer than the other and one had the shape of a round lump in the middle of the street.

Tiffany saw them walking toward her as she nodded her head and returned her police radio to her duty belt. "I'm so glad you could both meet me here. What a confusing crime scene."

Cory said, "Were there two bodies?"

Tiffany pointed toward the smaller area. "No, the one off to the left is the head. Somebody drained the blood from the body and then apparently felt the need to cut off the head."

"Were there any puncture-like wounds in the neck?" Marie strained her eyes from the sun as she watched the forensic team take samples and place them in evidence bags.

"Not on this victim, but someone drained his blood. We can't figure out if that occurred before or after the head was cut off." Tiffany nodded at one of the men from the forensic team and then looked back at Marie. "I was hoping you could do the same thing as you did before with his wallet. It didn't have any identification, but maybe you can learn something with that psychometry thing you do."

"Sure, I'll be glad to give it a try." Marie followed Tiffany toward the crime scene tape and stopped short when she spotted the victim's pinky toe sticking out from under the sheet. She quickly turned her head and took the evidence bag from Tiffany containing the wallet.

"I'll just walk over to the other side of the street if you don't mind. I'd like a little privacy." Marie nodded at Cory to follow her toward a bench and then sat down.

Cory sat next to Marie and grabbed her knee. "Are you okay to do this?"

"Yeah, I just wanted to sit down this time and thought it would be best to have you close by, so I don't fall over and hit my head."

Tiffany crossed the street and stood off to the side as Marie carefully held the evidence bag in both of her hands. She gingerly ran her fingers against the wallet and closed her eyes. Her breathing slowed down, and her ears began to ring when instantly a man swung a curved bladed object aimlessly in the air. She felt his fear and tried to make sense of the scene playing out in front of her.

Before Marie could get a glance at his attacker, she heard a loud engine sound, and the darkness became illuminated with bright lights from an industrial tractor. She then witnessed the man being dragged by a chain behind the tractor across a field covered in corn. The engine stopped, and the man was bloodied and had become unconscious.

The next vision clip was of the man lying on the ground with his arms shielding his face. He let out a blood-curdling scream when Marie saw the sharp bladed tool come down to his neck. Marie jolted awake and realized she was still on the bench leaning against Cory's shoulder.

"Marie, are you okay? You didn't move much this

time." Cory was ready with the bottled water as he removed the cap and handed it to her.

Marie took the bottle and chugged half of it down and then handed it back to him. "Thanks, and this man wasn't murdered by vampires."

Tiffany moved closer to Marie and pulled out her notebook and began writing. "Why do you say that?"

"Because this man was tied up to a tractor and dragged through a cornfield. He was fighting, at first, for dear life swinging some curved blade. Unfortunately, that blade is what was used to cut off his head. I couldn't see his attackers. How he ended up here, I have no clue."

Tiffany returned her notebook to her shirt pocket and extended her hand to Marie. "Thanks again. You've given us something to go on. This gentleman may be a farmer, and there's one farm I know of that has a cornfield."

Marie shook Tiffany's hand. "You're welcome. Is there anything we can do?"

"I'll keep you both posted." Tiffany then shook Cory's hand. "Thanks again, I appreciate this."

Marie watched Detective Captain Hayes walk back to one of her deputies and then they both got into a squad car and drove off. "That was a horrific vision I just had. This poor guy."

"Let's give Gale a call to see where they are and then you need to take a rest. You know how this drains you."

"Okay, I don't see any text messages from her yet. They may still be with the general." Marie held onto Cory's arm as they made their way back to the SUV.

Marie couldn't shake the feeling of being watched as she looked around in all directions trying to catch the perpetrator. Not having control over a situation made her even more uneasy.

MARIE AND CORY met up with the team at the carriage houses. They discussed what took place at the crime scene and Marie explained how the victim was murdered and had his head cut off.

Isabella shivered and popped a chip into her mouth. "Ugh, let's not talk about people getting their heads cut off. I had enough of that last month."

Gale said, "I agree. Do you think his murder had anything to do with vampires?"

"No, we don't." Marie poured herself a glass of chardonnay and grabbed some cheese and crackers and sat next to Gail. "None of this is making any sense. Why would I see this man dragged behind a tractor? And why did they cut off his head?"

"Not to change the subject, but Margaret told me some good news. She was able to set up a meeting with Mr. Pride. Remember him from the ball?" Mimi shoved Jim over on the love seat and continued eating her grapes.

"Oh yeah, he was kind of creepy. I didn't like the way he wore his mask. It was as if it were upside down on his face." Isabella grabbed more chips and set them on her plate.

Mimi said, "According to Margaret, Alexander is a very well-respected gentleman in the community. He works tirelessly for the city and donates much of his time and money to their charities. He's agreed to meet us around seven this evening at his law office on Bull Street. Margaret said she'll meet us there."

Harry lumbered over to the kitchen sink and filled

his glass with water. "Is everyone forgetting about the possibility of our first victim turning tonight? As the general stated, this would be the allotted timeframe."

Cory replied, "I haven't forgotten. I talked with Tim earlier and asked him to tag along with me for a bit of a stake-out."

"Kind of an odd stake-out, don't you think?" Gale finished the glass of merlot and grabbed the bottle and poured another.

"Yes, you could say that, considering I'm usually staking out a live person, but I don't see any other way. The general has agreed to lend us each a sword and stake, just in case." Cory caught Marie's look and casually grabbed her knee. "I promise we'll be careful."

"You'd better be because if anything happens to you, I'll kill ya." Gale saw everyone's stare as she continued, "Yeah I know, I heard it the minute I said it."

Tim chuckled as he pulled Gale against his neck and kissed her on the top of her head. "Always looking out for me, aren't you?"

Marie finished her glass of wine and set her glass on the counter. "Let's finish dinner and get ourselves organized to talk with Mr. Pride. We'll all need to stay in touch, especially Tim and Cory."

THIRTEEN

Cory and Tim took their vampire hunting tools and left for the morgue, while Marie and the rest of the team made their way to Bull Street. Marie didn't feel as though she was being watched anymore, which gave her a sense of relief and fear at the same time. She pushed the fear out of her mind and telepathically asked for continued protection from her spirit guides.

They jammed themselves into one SUV and then drove down Gaston Street past Forsyth Park when Marie looked through the moss-hung oaks and spotted the bright white painted cast iron water fountain spraying water into its basin.

She remembered reading there was a total of twenty-four parks created and spaced every few blocks in the city. Each park displayed their character with beautiful spaces to sit and relax and admire the architecture along the streets, which consisted of Federal, Georgian, and Gothic Revival buildings, to name a few.

They parked in front of the simple tan brick law firm building, and everyone haphazardly exited the

SUV looking like a clown car in a circus. Margaret was waiting inside and waved to them from the lobby. Marie kept Isabella close as she led the way into the building and found the elevator and pushed the button. While Marie waited for the doors to open, she looked around the foyer and thought it was a bit mundane. The elevator bell dinged, the team all huddled in at once, and they made their way to the fifth floor.

Marie got caught off-guard when the doors opened to a luxurious reception area, which was in complete contradiction of the rest of the building. The soft mint walls were calming and pleasing to the eye, as was the cherry office furniture. The opulent tan velvet settee apparently hadn't been used because there were no indentations in the cushion.

Margaret pointed toward the conference room to the right, which they could see through the wall of windows that lined the reception area. There was no receptionist; in fact, the office was a deafening silence. Marie spotted Alexander Pride scouring over papers when he sensed them staring through the glass. He still wore his blue-tinted wire-rimmed glasses, and his raven hair was slicked back making him a perfect doppelgänger of Orlando Bloom.

Alexander waved them in and pushed his files to the side. "Good evening everyone, so nice to see you all again. Please, come in and have a seat. Help yourselves to some coffee, tea, and scones on the credenza."

Margaret smiled and leaned toward Alexander and allowed him to kiss her cheek. "It's so kind of you to meet with us. We know how busy you are."

Marie pulled out an oversized oak chair that displayed a golden paisley fabric and set her cell phone down on the opulent matching oak table. "Yes, it is very kind of you to meet with us. We promise not to take up too much of your time."

Alexander looked through his blue-tinted glasses and gave Marie a lazy smile. "Nonsense, I'm about done with these briefs. I suspect we're going to be talking about vampires."

Isabella sat next to Marie and arranged her tea and scone on a napkin in front of her. "Yes, I've been dying to learn how you know about the so-called vampire community. Have you met some?"

"Yes, I have. I've been an attorney for a few." Alexander leaned back in his chair and stared a hole through Isabella. "Unfortunately, there are some things I can't discuss as their attorney, but I'll answer as many of your questions as I can."

After everyone made their introductions, Marie pulled out the journal from her purse and set it on the table. "Do you mind if I take notes of our discussion? It helps us to process the events."

"Be my guest." Alexander gracefully set his pen on top of the stack of files and gave his attention to Marie.

"I guess the first question I have, have you heard about the pig that was slaughtered on the Tanners' farm and do you think any of that had to do with vampires?"

"I did hear about the unfortunate occurrence. I know the Tanners personally, and the loss of that pig causes a great deal of hardship for them. They're trying to run a business, and that's part of their livelihood." Alexander glanced around the table and then rested his eyes again on Marie. "As far as a vampire doing the slaughtering, I'm not sure. I don't believe it lines up with the way a vampire sates its need for blood. Although, what Elizabeth saw may have been a vampire feeding on the animal after the fact."

Isabella stopped in mid-chew and said, "What do you mean?"

Alexander replied, "If a vampire is hungry enough, and is trying to remain in the code of its coven, it'll find any way that it can to feed. Their sense of smell is uncanny due to the high sensitivity of the vomeronasal organ, which is a small sac on either side of the nasal septum, containing receptor cells that pick up chemical signals, pheromones if you will, from other organisms."

Jim remained rigid in his chair as he casually took a sip of coffee and waited for a lull in the conversation. "Tell me Mr. Pride, how is it you know so much detail about vampires?"

Alexander shifted his torso toward Jim and leaned further back in his chair. "Because, as I said, I have represented a few. There are also known cases dating back to the sixteen hundreds of murderers blaming vampirism for their heinous acts and bloodlust."

Gale giggled and stopped short when Alexander stared a hole right through her. "I'm sorry, I didn't mean to laugh, but did you say there are actual murder cases documented of people being killed by vampires?"

Alexander swiftly got up from his chair and glided over to the credenza and poured another cup of coffee. After adding cream and sugar, he turned and made his way back to his chair and sat down. "Yes, that is correct. I'm used to the skeptics. I believe we need to have some skepticism, but the things I've witnessed and the people I've met made me a believer."

Mimi squeezed the herbal tea bag of the remaining liquid and then set it on the saucer. "What are some of the cases?"

"Off the top of my head, there was the Vampire of Hanover, Fritz Haarmann. He was one of the world's first serial killers back in nineteen eighteen. For about six years he murdered two dozen people, many of them he killed by biting their necks."

Isabella couldn't sit any further on the front of her chair as she intently listened to Alexander. "What happened to him?"

"They sentenced him to death by guillotine, and I believe his head was preserved in a jar for scientists to study." Alexander took another sip of his coffee and slowly looked around the room.

Gale squinched her face. "That's disgusting."

Harry said, "I remember the case of Richard Chase. He went on a murder spree, and they tagged him with the name of The Vampire of Sacramento. I believe this took place in nineteen seventy-eight. He murdered his victims between the ages of two and thirty-six years, disemboweled them, and then drank their blood."

Jim shook his head and dropped his scone on his plate. "He murdered babies?"

Alexander replied, "Yes, and without going into any more detail of six or more cases, you can see why I'm not sure what happened to the pig."

Marie hastily finished writing her notes and looked at Alexander. "What do you think happened to the woman found on the beach?"

"I heard about that, and I must say that seems to

fit more of the mold of being murdered by a vampire, but it could have been made to look like a vampire." Alexander finished his coffee and pushed his cup away from his files and continued, "I also don't believe a vampire killed the gentleman who had his head chopped off."

Marie replied, "He wasn't." She caught herself and continued, "At least that's what I think."

Alexander slyly looked over his glasses and smiled that lazy smile. "How did you come up with that reasoning? If you don't mind me asking."

Marie darted her eyes around the room and carefully weighed her words. "My husband, Cory, is a police officer and he has been in touch with the captain. He agrees with your theory."

"I see, well is there anything else you would like to know?" Alexander looked at Margaret and smiled. "Margaret, we do need to have dinner and discuss our next event. It's going to be an important one."

Margaret stood up from her chair and smiled. "Yes, I agree. Okay, everyone, I think we need to let Alexander get back to his work. We've taken up enough of his time."

Isabella frowned and slid her chair back and folded her arms. "I thought you were going to introduce us or tell us more about the vampire community. Didn't you say you met some who believe they are vampires?"

Alexander stood up in a stealth-like manner and began putting files away in a tall oak filing cabinet. "That would depend on whether they wanted to meet you or not. They don't care for anyone mocking them, and they certainly don't welcome skeptics."

"I'm not a skeptic." Isabella stood up and walked

over to where Alexander was standing. "We're a paranormal investigative team, we believe in the unexplained."

Alexander turned and rested his hand on Isabella's shoulder. "You're quite persistent, aren't you? Very well, I'll get in touch with Margaret if I can come up with a meeting for you. I won't promise anything."

Marie felt uneasy with Alexander's hand resting on Isabella's shoulder as she made her way to Isabella and gently grabbed her elbow. "Come on Isabella. We'll let Mr. Pride get back to his work."

Alexander turned toward the team and said, "It was nice meeting all of you. I wish you all good luck with helping the Tanners. Margaret, I'll call you tomorrow?"

"Yes, that would be fine." Margaret hurriedly moved everyone out of the conference room and into the reception area.

"What's the big hurry all of a sudden?" Gale tried to avoid jamming into Marie's back as she followed everyone out toward the elevator.

Margaret hit the button and looked at Gale. "I could sense it was time to go. Alexander was getting a bit impatient. I think he gets uncomfortable with people knowing he has associations with the so-called vampire community."

"I think we got enough information and Alexander's point of view sheds a little more light on the latest murders." Marie followed the team into the elevator when her cell phone rang. "This must be Cory."

"Ask him to tell Tim that I need my lip gloss. I left it in his pants pocket." Gale ignored Marie's glare and rolled her eyes.

Marie answered the phone as they made their way to the first floor and out of the elevator when she stopped in mid-stride and started waving at everyone. "Cory, I'm going to put you on speaker phone so that everyone can hear you. Would you please repeat what you just said to me?"

"I said that the female victim is gone."

Gale yelled into the speaker. "What do you mean she's gone?"

"When Tim and I arrived, we saw Tiffany talking to the ME, and they shared with us the identity of both of the victims. The woman's name is Candy Bucket from Maine and was traveling here on vacation. The male vic, Ted Hardcastle, was a local farmer here in Savannah." There was a brief silence, and then Cory continued, "I asked Tiffany if we could see Candy's body and when the ME pulled the drawer of her cold chamber, it was empty."

Jim asked, "How is that even possible? Did she transition into a vampire?"

Cory replied, "We have no idea, and they're all as baffled as we are. Plus, this Ted Hardcastle's property is the neighboring farm to the Tanners. They're questioning some of the staff now, but Tim and I thought we'd meet up with you."

"We were just going to head back to the carriage house. I wonder if there's some correlation between these two farms?" Marie saw a shadow and quickly turned toward Isabella. "Cory, can you hold on a minute? Isabella, did you just see that shadow?"

"Yes, it's Gracie. She's acting quite hysterical. She wants me to follow her."

Mimi stood motionless next to Margaret and

looked around the room as if waiting to see the shadow. "Follow her where?"

Isabella replied, "I don't know."

Marie turned off the cell phone speaker and held it up to her ear. "Cory, we'll wait for you here. By the time you arrive, maybe we'll have a better idea where Gracie is asking us to go."

SHE HEARD his deep voice whisper her name as she glided along the muddy path. The cool night air seemed to blow right through her as the sounds of insects chewing hammered in her ears. She picked up the scent of a raccoon's blood from under a shrub, increasing her need to feed, as she made her way down the crypt stairs.

When she arrived, he was waiting for her with open arms. "I have been waiting for you. Come to me, my child. You are now a member of my coven."

She hastily followed him further into the underground concrete halls and stopped at a mantle draped in white satin. Lying on top was a lifeless deer freshly killed by a car.

She saw the cold eyes and smiled as she looked at her master. "Is it for me?"

"Yes, my love, you need to feed to keep up your strength. This animal lost its life. Enjoy your first feeding." He stepped back into the shadows and watched her plunge her mouth on the deer's neck. "Take your time and allow your digestion to settle. Remember, this is only the beginning, and I am here to protect you."

The incessant slurping echoed throughout the crypt as the fledgling drank the deer's blood. She felt her master's hand on her arm as he gently pulled her away and handed her a satin handkerchief.

"Come, we have many things to do. You can come back again and feed when it is time."

THE TEAM PARKED in front of the Bonaventure Cemetery's gate and quietly got out of their SUVs, and one-by-one waited by the fence. The graveyard lost the appeal it had during the day as the moss looked like cobwebs dripping from the live oak branches.

Mimi pulled the zipper up on her sweater and continued to look around as if waiting for something to jump out. "I'm not sure if this is a good idea. We could have contacted someone to let us in."

Cory was the first to climb over as he helped the rest of the team descend to the ground. "I've put a call into Tiffany to let her know what we were doing. She's on standby if we need her help, and the cops patrolling this area are aware of it also."

Marie made sure Isabella was next to her as she shined her flashlight on the concrete pathway. "Isabella, can you see Gracie?"

"I did when we first pulled up, but I think she disappeared down the path on the left." Isabella pointed her flashlight in the opposite direction.

Tim was the last to climb over the fence as he made his way next to Gale. "Are we ready to roll?"

Gale replied, "As ready as I'll ever be. You'd think we'd get used to doing this stuff, but no, you don't. I don't blame Margaret for going home. It was probably a little too freaky for her."

Harry pushed his glasses up his nose and retrieved the vial of holy water from his vest pocket and held it tightly in his hand. "She seemed a bit nervous when she realized Isabella was serious about seeing Gracie."

"Yeah well, not everyone can wrap their heads around seeing people talk to the dead." Marie shrugged her shoulders and then followed Cory and Isabella down the path and into the bowels of the cemetery.

Jim stood next to Mimi as his hand rested on her lower back. "Everyone needs to stay alert. I wish we had some of those stakes from the general."

Tim replied, "I wish I had his gun."

They continued following the road and eventually made their way to a wrought iron gated fence surrounding a tombstone of a little girl perched on top in a seated position. She was almost life-like as the name displayed Gracie on the front.

"This is it. The statue looks the same as Gracie in my vision." Isabella peered through the wrought iron balusters and shined her flashlight on statue's angelic face.

"Can you see her anywhere?" Marie walked over and stood next to Isabella and stared at the statue.

"No, I don't know where she is."

Gale shook her head and shoved her fists on her hips. "Great, we're in a creepy cemetery at night chasing a ghost, and you've lost her."

"She'll find me when she's ready, but I am getting the sense that we need to head over in that direction." Isabella moved away from the fence and pointed her flashlight to another mausoleum replicating a mini gothic cathedral.

Cory gazed in the direction Isabella pointed and squinted his eyes. "I think I see someone over there."

Gale said, "Don't tell me you're seeing ghosts now."

"No, I see a figure that looks to be holding a torch."

"Who do you think it is?" Harry started walking toward the figure as the rest of the group followed.

"Harry, slow down, we don't want to spook whoever it is." Marie held onto Isabella's elbow with her right hand as her left clutched the vial of holy water in the pocket of her jacket.

Tim said, "Maybe it's a vampire."

"Carrying a torch?" Mimi grabbed onto Jim's hand and remained alert to her surroundings as her heart pounded in her chest.

Marie felt Isabella jerk around, almost pulling her down onto the ground. "Isabella what are you doing?"

"I just saw Gracie. She's over there by that figure."

As quietly as possible, they made their way toward the shadows dancing off the tombstones and eventually found themselves watching a man wearing a cloak unlock the green oxidized brass door to the mausoleum.

"Who are you?" Marie pursed her lips in frustration and watched the figure jump in fear as he dropped the torch and then turned to face them.

Cory quickly picked up the torch and stamped out the burning embers in the grass. "I think we need to be a little more careful."

FOURTEEN

"**Hello everyone.** What brings you here this evening?" Baron breathed a sigh of relief and wiped his brow with his sleeve.

Gale pushed her way in front of everyone and stood next to Baron as her five-foot-nine frame towered over his. "What are we doing here? I think the real question is, what are you doing here?"

"I believe Carmilla's hiding place is here."

Cory walked over to the sack and started retrieving the swords and stakes. "And you didn't feel it was necessary to contact us?"

Baron pointed at Isabella. "I felt it was too dangerous and I didn't want her to give our chase away to Carmilla."

Gale glared at Baron and then grabbed a stake from Cory. "That's a bit rude, don't you think?"

"I apologize, but I needed to be sure, and I couldn't take any chances of losing her this time. But now that you are here, will you join me?"

Isabella walked over to Baron and smiled. "Yes, we would. And I happen to agree with you because Gracie has led us here."

"Who is Gracie?"

Marie replied, "It's a long story, and I don't think I want Isabella going with us."

"It's better than staying out here. Besides, Gracie wants me to follow her. She's waiting on the other side of the door."

Baron looked toward the door in confusion and then continued fiddling with the lock. "This shouldn't take me long."

"Okay, you can come with us, but please stay close to us. Do you understand?" Marie shook Isabella's shoulders and gave her a motherly scowl.

"Yes, I understand, and we need to hurry. Gracie is in a total panic."

Baron clicked the lock open and pushed the heavy metal door open as far as he could remaining careful not to drop the lit torch and proceeded inside. "I'm not going to try and figure out who Gracie is, but I suspect she may know where Carmilla is hiding."

The team again found themselves walking through the dark, dank crypt swinging their torches and flashlights in all directions. They had to be sure no bloodsuckers were hiding in wait. Marie's heart was pounding in her chest as she kept an eye on Isabella and tried to see the difference between the small patches of light and darkness.

Tim remained close to Gale and edged closer to Cory as he darted his torch around his head. "Cory, please tell me you have your off-duty gun on you."

"As a matter of fact, I do. Not quite sure what it'll do against vampires, but it's locked and loaded."

Baron stopped everyone and held up his hand to remain still and whispered, "I hear something up ahead."

Harry replied, "I hear it too. It sounds like a muffled conversation."

Isabella grabbed Marie's elbow and leaned in toward her ear and spoke softly. "Marie, can you see Gracie up ahead?"

Marie strained her eyes in the dark and caught the shadow of little Gracie. "Yes, I do see her. She's pleading for us to follow her."

"We don't know what's up ahead. If it were vampires, wouldn't they be on us by now? I mean they're supposed to have this keen sense of hearing, right?" Gale backed up against Tim and continued to look back for fear of anyone attacking from behind.

Mimi tried to keep her arm from shaking as she raised the stake in her left hand and grabbed hold of Jim's hand with the other. "Standing here isn't answering any of our questions. I think we need to keep going."

Baron waved his hand for the team to follow him as he instinctively touched his pistol resting on his hip. "I agree, let's keep moving but remain quiet and cautious."

Marie huddled Isabella between her and Cory and continued straining her eyes to see what was up ahead. She refused to look down and see what was crunching under her feet when out of nowhere a shrilled scream echoed through the tunnel and everyone took off in a full-blown run.

Cory's cop instincts kicked in as he waved everyone to place their backs against the wall before they made the next turn. He carefully peered around the corner, reached for his gun, and yelled, "Stop where you are, this is the police."

Gale yelled, "What the hell is he doing? We don't have any backup."

In a chaotic frenzy, there was gunfire echoing as bullets ricocheted off the walls and everyone dropped on all fours and covered their heads. Marie threw her stake on the ground as she laid her body over Isabella and tried to protect her from getting shot.

Cory and Baron returned fire as bodies up ahead began to drop from being hit. The gunfire stopped and off in the distance a voice yelled, "We give up. Don't shoot."

Cory got up from his knees and looked back at the group. "Tim, Baron, and Jim come with me. The rest of you stay here."

Cory walked two feet when a young woman wearing jean overalls and a straw hat came running at him screaming at the top of her lungs. She landed in Cory's arms and began to sob. Marie stood up and helped her over to where they were crouched and tried to calm her down.

"What's your name? Are you okay? Have you been hurt?" Marie tried to settle the woman as her body shook in Marie's embrace.

"My name is Chelsea McFarland. I didn't get shot, but they were going to kill me."

Harry looked at the two men that surrendered and then pushed his drooping glasses up his nose. "Who are they?"

"I don't know who they are. I was working in the field at the Tanners when out of nowhere they grabbed me from behind. They were wearing hoods and stupid masks. They kept telling me they were going to sacrifice me for the good of the cause. The next think I knew I was here at the cemetery. None of it made any sense, but they had these tools and equipment down in another part of this crypt. It looked like some primitive science lab. They were going to hook me up to a machine and drain my blood."

Marie continued to hold the woman as she sobbed into her chest. "Can someone please find out what's going on up there?"

Cory yelled out, "It's okay, you can all come here. We have two of them restrained."

Gale asked, "What about the rest?"

Baron replied in his formal British accent. "They're dead."

Marie arrived first and immediately hugged Cory around the neck and then saw two dead men lying on the muddy ground and two others sitting against the wall handcuffed to each other. "What the hell were they doing?"

"From what I can make out, these gentleman work for a Mr. John Evans and they have been trying to get the Tanners to sell their land. Apparently, Mr. Evan's land is smacked up against the Tanners and the Hardcastle's properties. He wants to build a multi-billion-dollar development, and this apparently is his idea of getting his way." Cory's gun remained aimed at the men sitting on the ground.

Jim shined his flashlight on the dead bodies and quickly looked away. "Couldn't they have just asked them to sell?"

The blond goon picked his head up from his knees and shifted trying to twist his hand out of the handcuffs. "They refused to sell. That pissed Evans off, so we came up with a plan to scare them into selling."

Chelsea pushed away from Marie and glared at

the suspects. "So you had to kill our pigs and Mr. Hardcastle?"

"You fools wouldn't listen to reason, so yeah, we did what was necessary."

Isabella said, "Including an innocent woman?"

The blond suspect looked at her with a blank stare and shook his head. "We didn't kill no woman. We only killed the pig and Hardcastle. He wasn't supposed to die. We were only trying to scare him. He must have had a heart attack."

Cory asked, "Why the hell did you cut off his head?"

"We tried to make it look like a vampire killed him, but it got kind of messy, so we just cut off his head instead. We thought it would confuse the cops and keep them off our backs."

"So, we still don't know who killed that woman from Maine?" Mimi shook her head and then leaned against the damp stones of the wall.

Baron continued pointing his gun at the suspects. "I guess we don't."

Gale asked, "What do we do with them now?"

"I called Tiffany, and they're on their way. It shouldn't take long." Cory looked at Isabella and said, "Isabella, are you okay?"

"It's Gracie. She wants us to follow her into that wall."

Gale asked, "The wall, and how do you suppose we do that?"

"I don't know, but she's obviously got something else to show us."

Marie turned her head toward the other end of the tunnel and spotted lights coming their way. "I think the police are here."

"Good, now we can get out of here and get ready to go home. I could use a drink." Gale set her stake down against Tim's leg and adjusted her jeans.

Isabella moved in front of Marie and pointed toward the wall. "Can you see Gracie? She doesn't want us to leave."

Marie adjusted her sight and then looked at Isabella. "I'm not sure what else we can do here. Now that we understand what happened to the pig. The police can take it from here."

"Didn't you tell me that your spirit guides said there were two kinds of vampires? These were obviously the fake ones but just as dangerous. Please, Marie, we have to follow this through. You know Gracie won't leave me alone until we do."

Marie turned toward Cory and shrugged her shoulders. "What do you think?"

"I think we wait until the police take these perps first. As far as the rest, I leave that up to the team."

The police arrived and took the two men into custody and continued marking the scene with crime tape. After all the questions had been asked and answered, the team moved off to the side to discuss the next step.

Marie said, "Okay, it's eight to one in favor of staying here to see what Gracie is trying to tell us."

Gale rolled her eyes and picked up her stake. "Whatever, let's get this over with."

Isabella closed her eyes and began to communicate with Gracie through telepathy when she quickly walked over to the other end of the tunnel and started to push on the stones in the wall. "There's a secret doorway here."

"Seriously?" Gale ignored Marie's look and walked toward Isabella.

Marie wanted to support Isabella in her quest and began pushing on stones next to her and then suddenly stopped. "Isabella, I believe you are correct."

"Why do you say that?"

"Because my spirit guides just showed up and look here, this stone is loose." Marie turned around and looked at Tim. "Can you help me push this please?"

Tim walked over and gave it a shove, and within seconds a small section of the wall began to move inward allowing just enough space for someone to slither through. "I'll be damned."

"I told you." Impatient as always, Isabella started to go through until Marie grabbed her. "Why are you stopping me?"

"Because you aren't going in first. Let Baron and Cory go through please, then you can follow us." Marie pulled Isabella out of the way and waited until Baron and Cory disappeared behind the wall.

The team followed each other single file into the narrow, hidden passage, trying to keep their torches lit to see what was around them. It smelled of decay, and the walls were wet to the touch. The tunnel seemed to go on forever until Baron finally entered a large opening at the end.

"I think we're in another section. From what I can see it looks like a crypt room." Baron walked over to the side of one wall and placed his torch on a fixture as it caught fire.

The primitive room illuminated and exposed a ceiling height of no more than six and a half feet. There were two arched tunnels up ahead leading in opposite directions giving the impression of a cathedral.

Harry carefully walked into one of the tunnels and held his torch out in front of him. "Which tunnel do we take?"

"I almost hate to say it, but should we split up?" Jim walked over to the other tunnel and shivered and then came back to the center of the group.

Cory replied, "I'm not sure that's a good idea."

"I don't think we have to split up." Isabella walked over next to Harry.

"I have to agree with Isabella." Marie stood next to her and pointed toward the empty darkness. "Gracie and my spirit guides want us to accompany them down this tunnel."

Baron released his pistol from its holster and put it in his right hand while holding the torch in the other. "I think we'd better get ourselves prepared for what's on the other end of this tunnel."

Gale said, "Are we going to do this?"

Tim pulled Gale against his chest and kissed her forehead. "It looks that way."

They were able to move two by two as Baron and Cory led the way. Tim and Jim brought up the rear. They remained silent as they cautiously made their way down the tunnel all the while keeping a close hand on their tools for defense against the unknown.

Baron spotted a dim light up ahead as he put up his torch hand to bring them to a halt. He turned and motioned for them to be aware of the possible danger ahead and then continued walking with his back against the wall.

Cory followed suit and just as they were ready to make the turn, he spotted something out of the corner of his left eye and swiftly turned his torch in its direction and shouted. "Everyone look out!"

Within seconds ghoul-like soldiers were running toward them with pale skin and dark eyes. Everyone got into defense mode and began swinging their stakes and swords trying to ward off the chance of suffering sudden death from a vampire.

Marie pulled Isabella with her against the wall and tried to take in the scene that was playing out in front of her. She was able to see a woman at the other end of the room screaming and barking orders. She squinted to get a better look in the midst of all the chaos and yelled to Isabella. "That woman looks like Margaret."

Before she got the last words out, a rush of men came to their defense and started slaying and thrashing bodies against the walls. The SIPS team gathered in a huddle and tried to keep themselves safe, while Baron kept shooting in all directions.

Mimi pointed to one of the men and tried to scream above the chaos. "I think that beast is Alexander Pride. Why does his face keep changing? What's he doing here?"

Gale was shaking and trying to keep her stake steady. "Marie, that woman who looks like Margaret. Is her face changing too?"

Baron turned toward the woman after hearing Gale and froze in his stance. "Dear God, that's Carmilla?"

Isabella poked her head out from under Marie's arm and screamed. "Margaret's a vampire?"

Within minutes the ghouls disappeared out the other end of the room down another tunnel, and the place fell silent. The only people who remained were

Alexander Pride and a group of men all wearing clothes that looked like they had stepped out of a Blade movie.

Cory immediately turned around to check on his wife and the team and then found himself face to face with someone that appeared to be Alexander Pride. "Do you mind telling me what the hell just happened and why you're here?"

Alexander set his sword back in its sheath and gave his lazy smile. "I would assume it's obvious. We just saved your asses."

Marie asked, "From what?"

"From vampires, of course." Alexander walked over to Baron and lifted the old gentleman up off the ground. "Hello Baron, we meet again. I see you're still trying to kill Carmilla."

FIFTEEN

Baron tried to catch his breath and continued to lean on Alexander. "Serafino, good to see you, my friend. She had me completely deceived. I feel like such a fool."

"You're not a fool, old friend. Carmilla found my coven. She confronted me, but I was able to trick her."

Baron asked, "How did you do that?"

"I was able to shapeshift into another human. She almost discovered me, but I kept my wits about me."

Gale ignored their hardy laughter and brushed the grime from her jeans and stood next to Baron and looked directly at the man in the blue-tinted glasses. "I thought your name was Alexander."

"It is, but Serafino was my given name."

Cory realized he was still holding his gun and slowly holstered it back into place on his hip. "Would you please explain what the hell just happened and who are these dead men?"

Isabella said, "Yeah, they all don't look like real vampires."

"A few of them are, but the others are not." Alexander looked around at the dead bodies and then continued, "As I said, my given name is Serafino, but I haven't used that name since the nineteenth century. I met up with Baron here when his niece was turned by the same beast who turned my father."

"You're a vampire?" Isabella slowly stood behind Marie and kept her eye on Alexander.

"More or less, I'm what they call a dhampir. My father was a vampire, and my mother was human. She died in childbirth. My grandparents raised me. I grew normally until adulthood. When I reached the age of eighteen, I noticed my senses became more acute, and my strength and speed were supernatural."

Harry asked, "You're able to walk in the daylight and are also immortal?"

Serafino began picking up the bodies and dumped them in a pile and then grabbed the torch from Harry and set them on fire. He ignored the shrill burning sounds and looked back at the group. "Yes, that is correct."

Jim tried to peel Mimi's clenched hand from his arm. "What made you become a vampire hunter?"

"Obligation, I suppose. After learning what vampires are capable of and how my mother died, I became repulsed at the idea of living off another human. I'm able to eat normal foods, and I only crave blood on occasion. I won't go into an explanation on that subject. Over the years I've adopted those who were turned and lost. I've established my coven, and I'm very protective of my fledglings. It's not easy disciplining them." Serafino thought of Nicolai and smiled.

Marie shielded her eyes from the inferno and continued to keep Isabella behind her back. "So who are these men?"

"Some are wannabe vampires who got fooled by Margaret, also known as, Carmilla. I had tracked her here and gained her trust. She wasn't aware of who I was until our meeting at my office. She spotted the tattoo molnija mark on my neck sticking out from under my collar." Serafino stared into the fire and continued, "I am considered a guardian but was cast out from my Moroi coven."

Mimi spoke for the first time and tried to keep her voice from cracking. "Why?"

"That's another story, and I don't have the time to explain." Serafino shook Baron's hand and slapped him on the back. "My friend, I'm sorry I couldn't take Carmilla down. Maybe we need to take you back to your time and try to come up with a better plan."

The general graciously smiled and shook his head. "I'm not sure I have any more fight left in me. I'm not immortal like you Serafino. But I do believe I need to be heading back. I'll need to wait for the next solstice. In the meantime, we can share the journey, and I'll give you as much information as I can."

Isabella slowly came out from behind Marie. "Are you still in your shapeshifting form?"

Serafino winked at Isabella. "Yes, I don't think you want to see me as I am."

Tim emerged from the group and looked at Serafino. "So you nor Carmilla had anything to do with the death of the pigs or the farmer?"

"No, I'm disappointed in my youngest, Nicolai. The pig was slaughtered by someone else, and his craving took the best of him." Serafino looked at Marie and Isabella. "I know of your gifts. Please beware and always be cautious. I believe Carmilla will take her vengeance and one never knows who will be on the other end of her retribution."

Cory walked in front of Marie shielding her from Alexander. "So how do you explain the dead woman found on Tybee Island?"

Serafino lazily smiled and moved closer to Cory as their noses nearly touched and he spoke in a whisper. "I must confess. She was one of my donors. However, my Nicolai took matters into his own hands and turned her. As I said, I'm very protective of my coven. She will remain with me, and I will have to train her, as I've had to do with so many others."

Gale shivered and walked next to Marie and Isabella in a protective like manner. "So now what do we do?"

Serafino backed away from Cory, grabbed a stake, and proceeded to stir the ashes around from the body remains. "I would suggest you all go back to your homes and try to forget any of this happened. There'll be no proof of these bodies, and you have the men who tried to run those folks off their farms. As far as the woman found on the beach, now gone missing, just pass it off as crazy body snatchers."

Marie nodded and walked over to where Serafino stood as she took in his six-foot-nine stature and muscular physique. "Nobody would believe us anyway. Serafino or Alexander, I'd like to thank you for coming to our defense. I must say I never believed in vampires, but I'm also the last person to ignore anything as paranormal. I'll also heed your advice."

Serafino turned and looked directly into Marie's eyes and gave his usual lazy grin. "I respect your power my mystic. You almost entered my donor's mind and saw me. Please be careful and remain vigilant in your defenses."

Marie allowed him to softly kiss her knuckles all the while trying to keep her body from shaking in his presence. "I will do the best that I can."

Baron smiled and walked over to Marie and rested his hand on her elbow. "Thank you and thank you all for your aid in helping me fight Carmilla. I'm going to return with Serafino. We have much to catch up on and discuss. I wish you safe travels and hope we never see each other again."

"Here, here...I need a drink." Gale hooked her hand in Tim's and waved her hand in the air. "Take care Baron, happy hunting."

Everyone said their goodbyes and made their way back through the narrow passages and out of the crypt and mausoleum. It was nearly morning as they walked back to the gate and climbed over the fence. They silently got into their SUVs and remained that way on the ride back to the carriage houses. No one spoke of what just happened. It was almost an unspoken agreement that on this occasion, it was best forgotten for now and to be brought up at a later time.

Marie found Bailey patiently waiting for them when they arrived as she graciously paid the dog sitter and then took him out to relieve his bladder. Nobody spoke a word as they decided to pack up and get ready to travel back to Sullivan's Island. It was evident that everyone was still in shock and couldn't believe they met real vampires and a time traveler.

Those that weren't driving slept, while Marie played the scene in the underground tomb over and over again in her head. She was still trying to convince herself that Alexander was a dhampir and that

Margaret was a shapeshifter from an actual vampire named Carmilla.

Cory briefly took his eyes off the road and looked at Marie. "What's rolling around in that head of yours?"

"Probably the same things that are rolling around in yours." Marie reached out and ran her thumb on his cheek. "I saw you on the phone before we left. Did you hear any more from Tiffany?"

"Yeah, they arrested Evans, and it looks as though they squashed the multi-billion-dollar development. She said the Tanners were elated to hear they arrested the men working for Evans. I think they're hoping to get back to normal. Whatever that is."

"I gave up a long time ago on what is supposed to be normal. It's a shame that Mr. Hardcastle lost his life because of their greed. I'll reach out to Barbara when we get home." Marie looked in the backseat at Bailey's head resting on Isabella while she slept, and then turned back around in her seat. "I'm worried about Isabella and the warning Serafino gave us. Cory, the demon came back and took Myra from us. You don't think that'll happen with Carmilla, do you?"

Cory reached over and gently squeezed Marie's hand. "I don't know, but after seeing Serafino in action and the way he spoke of his dedication to hunting for Carmilla, I'd like to think he'd be someone we could call. It looked like you two had a connection."

Marie smiled and leaned her head against the headrest. "You're not jealous, are you?"

"Of course not. I'd just kick his ass if he came anywhere near you." Cory winked and then placed his hand back on the steering wheel.

"I see, my knight in shining armor." Marie shifted her seat back and took off her jacket. "I wonder if Baron will make it back to his time. Did you ever think you'd meet a time traveler? I'm still trying to wrap my head around that one."

"After all that we've been through and everything that I've witnessed and experienced, I don't question it anymore. The thing that I find amazing is that Isabella was right the whole time."

"Yes, yes she was. I'm quite proud of her."

Marie settled her head back and closed her eyes and drifted off to sleep. Within minutes she found herself dreaming of a cold, dark room with dirt surrounding a tomb. The earth began to tremble around the coffin when a shrilled cackle screamed her name and echoed in her ears. She saw Carmilla holding Isabella in her arms while Gracie and her spirit guides frantically tried to pull Isabella from her grasp. Carmilla's fangs were inches away from Isabella when Marie abruptly awoke and instinctively grabbed her neck.

Cory asked, "Are you okay? You nearly jumped out of the seat."

"Yeah, yeah it was just a dream." Marie turned around to find Isabella still sleeping as she tried to keep her heart from exploding out of her chest. "It was just a dream."

Dear reader,

We hope you enjoyed reading *Savannah's Secret* Please take a moment to leave a review, even if it's a short one. Your opinion is important to us.

Discover more books by Robin Murphy at https://www.nextchapter.pub/authors/robin-murphy.

Want to know when one of our books is free or discounted? Join the newsletter at http://eepurl.com/bqqB3H

Best regards,

Robin Murphy and the Next Chapter Team

ABOUT THE AUTHOR

Robin Murphy has worked in the administrative, graphic design, desktop publishing, writing, and self-publishing realm for more than thirty-five years. She is currently a virtual admin and freelance writer for a local newspaper and magazine.

The first book in her paranormal mystery series is *Sullivan's Secret*, the second is *Secret of the Big Easy*, the third is *Federal City's Secret*, and the fourth is *Secret of Coffin Island*.

Robin has been a speaker on author platforms, self-publishing, and marketing. She has also written *A Complete "How To" Guide for Rookie Writers*, which is a very practical, hands-on and user-friendly book to enable a rookie writer to learn how to get their newly created work produced and available to readers, as well as, a comedic romance titled, *Point and Shoot for Your Life*, which was a ReadFree.Ly 2016 Best Indie Book Finalist.

You can find Robin's books on Amazon.

ALSO BY ROBIN MURPHY

Marie Bartek and the SIPS Team Series:

Sullivan's Secret

Secret of the Big Easy

Federal City's Secret

Secret of Coffin Island

A Complete How-To Guide For Rookie Writers

Point and Shoot for Your Life

Savannah's Secret
ISBN: 978-4-86747-861-5
Mass Market

Published by
Next Chapter
1-60-20 Minami-Otsuka
170-0005 Toshima-Ku, Tokyo
+818035793528

28th May 2021

Lightning Source UK Ltd.
Milton Keynes UK
UKHW040638180621
385737UK00001B/67